American Grief in Four Stages

Sadie Hoagland

AMERICAN GRIEF IN FOUR STAGES

Stories

WEST VIRGINIA UNIVERSITY PRESS

MORGANTOWN

ISBN
Paper 978-1-949199-21-5
Ebook 978-1-949199-22-2

Library of Congress Cataloging-in-Publication Data
Names: Hoagland, Sadie, author.
Title: American grief in four stages : stories / Sadie Hoagland.
Description: First edition. | Morgantown : West Virginia University Press, 2019.
Identifiers: LCCN 2019018438 | ISBN 9781949199215 (paperback) | ISBN
        9781949199222 (ebook)
Subjects: LCSH: Grief–United States–Fiction. | Short stories, American–21st
        century.
Classification: LCC PS3608.O157 A6 2019 | DDC 813/.6–dc23
LC record available at https://lccn.loc.gov/2019018438

Book and cover design by Than Saffel / WVU Press.
Cover illustration by Anna Vesna / Shutterstock.

*To my Mom who read me books
and my Dad who told me stories (some of them true),
with immense love and gratitude.*

Contents

Cavalier Presentations of
Heartbreaking News

*I*t was my birthday when I found out that all the birds were electric. Well, almost all of them: sparrows, kestrels, wrens, ravens, and so on. Little feathered drones. They had no nests, and flew on AAA batteries until they sputtered out and dropped dead like real birds, falling out of the sky. I don't know what they did after they dropped because my mother didn't know.

It was my birthday and my mother told me about the birds in my hometown in the same inappropriate way she delivered all matters of life and death: casually, standing across the kitchen island from me, with one hand on the back of her hip and the other hand waving a sauce-covered spoon. This is how she told me the neighbor, Mr. Blue, had died, and also how she told me she had cancer. This was her worst habit. This cavalier presentation of heartbreaking revisions of our world. She hadn't always done it, but developed it after my oldest brother came out of the closet. She told me about him like this, the sauce specking the counter; she told me what I already knew and I nodded and she continued talking as if nothing had been revealed, as if everyone always already knew everything and for this I blame my brother for telling her not only last, but two years after he told the rest of us. But that's his business.

On my birthday, my mother had been talking about my father's retirement party, what a smash it was, talking over a warm basil steam, when she saw me looking out the sink window behind her at a little bird. A wren-ish bird. I know little of bird identification. I know generally which are supposed to be small and which big, and am confident I could spot a bald eagle from a mile away, but I've never seen one in person before.

It was my father's retirement and then she saw me watching a bird and it was, "Oh, would you look at that? We get such a variety of birds in the backyard now that they've gone electric, who would have thought? I'm even beginning to think they sing more beautifully than the old ones, a little more bluesy."

I stared at her as she segued into gossip about an aunt in rehab and then I slowly pushed off the kitchen barstool and walked to the thin-glassed window. I watched another bird, a blood-red hummingbird, and tried to see what she was talking about. Did she mean that the electrical company did something to bring in new and more birds? Or did she mean that they were actually electric? I watched its tiny flight to see if I could see some mechanical stutter before I realized that all hummingbirds have fast blinking movements, machines or not. I tried to look around for other birds but saw none.

"Oh, you and the birds." My mother interrupted herself when she saw I wasn't listening to say this like it was a thing, me and the birds. As if I'd ever watched a bird in my life.

"They brought them in just after that plane crash last winter. Said it was a pilot program for airspace positivity. People were up in arms of course, but I didn't mind. I figure someday we'll be electric, so why fight it, right pumpkin?" She lightly poked her prosthetic breasts and smiled.

I shrugged and went back to my seat at the island, watching her cook across from me like she was in some kind of 1950's terrarium, spotless paisley apron and all, her mouth a gentle frown, and wondered aloud what they'd done with the real birds.

"Oh, don't ask me. I don't want to know. I like to think they sent them someplace new. Like Japan. With the watercolors."

She carried on then to fill me in on the gossip of her Breast Cancer Survivor support group and I looked out the window and felt old. Really a lot older, like I'd just turned ten years older rather than one year older and if I kept driving to my hometown for my next birthdays, thirty-two, thirty-three, thirty-four, if I even lived that long, I'd be the world's youngest octogenarian.

At least the news about the birds hadn't left me iced over inside like her cancer had, or sobbing across from her deadpan busybody face, like when she told me that Mr. Blue had died. I hadn't seen him in over a year when she told me it was something like heart failure that did it, if she was remembering right, shaking her head, waving her finger in a rhythm meant to jog her memory, not noticing that I had put my hand to my mouth. I had to get up, stumbling as she watched motionless, and go into my old bedroom, which was now a guest room/museum for her miniature glass animal collection, and really lose it.

The thing is I'd been in love with Mr. Blue. After I graduated from college, I moved back home for one last stifling summer. My mother was in chemo, and the house was hot because she was always cold, and I had to get out and so had taken to long, unthinking walks. On these walks I would see Mr. Blue out gardening—he had recently retired early from his job at the postal service—and I would stop to say hello. We had always been friendly, but when he found out that I had studied literature he began to invite me in, to loan me books, ask what I thought about certain classics like *Walden*. He was a handsome older man, not by everybody's standards but by mine. He had no salt-and-pepper hair nor did he have the cycling passion of some fit older men, but he did have deep black eyes and was still as thin as a teenager. He was tall too, and he kind of leaned forward into his height. Not a stoop, but something more active, like he was always looking over a precipice just beyond his feet.

He lived two doors down and across the street and kept the apostrophe shapes of lawn between his landscaping so manicured it looked like a mini-golf course. I should have known by the orderliness of each grass blade that I wasn't going to get him to consent to my "but I'm a consenting adult" spiel—which I delivered one sweaty afternoon in his kitchen after he'd given me the "you're so young" spiel, after I'd made a pass at him by reaching over behind him to get down a glass for water and letting my breasts push against him, topping it all off with a kiss on his left earlobe, even a little suck of it, to which he gasped.

He got the last word and it was "I don't think I could ever look your father in the eye again." Which I didn't think would be a problem since they mostly saw each other from across the street and not close enough that my father would detect any askew glance, but he was firm in his resistance.

But, predictably, that only made the love more intense and the lonely ache of my twin bed that summer, the one I'd slept in for so many years, all the worse. I began fantasizing about Mr. Blue and me, on the scare quotes of lawn that led to his porch, dangerously public about our love, me walking home after with hundreds of identically trimmed grass pieces pressed into my ass, itching.

Now on my birthday my mother was talking about Mr. Blue again, or his house, saying, "A new family moved into Mr. Blue's house. They seem nice, have older children, both have left home, though

I think one, the youngest, is back for the summer or something."
I nodded and asked what time dinner was. An hour, she said, give
or take. I told her I wanted to see these birds, and thought I might
get some exercise, to which she nodded once, a quick approval, and
told me to be back in forty-five minutes just in case dinner was
done sooner and I said okay but dinner was never done sooner.
Always later, usually by an hour or so.

I walked down the street, looking up at the sky and trees for
signs of bird life, real or invented. I was walking and looking up and
the clouds were moving with me but I won't claim I didn't know
myself to be walking almost directly to Mr. Blue's house. I wanted
to see the lawn shapes, and when I did I wasn't disappointed. They
were mowed but not trimmed, cut but not buzzed.

I absentmindedly walked closer to the edges, taking slow steps
along the seam of the lawn, looking at how uneven the grass grew
when allowed to.

I didn't notice I was being watched.

"Did you lose something?" He spoke from just under the eaves
of the porch, where I had spent time with Mr. Blue after that day
in his kitchen; he had no longer invited me in, we'd just sat on the
porch steps and talked, as if he didn't trust me or him and so we
were going to be chaperoned by his front yard. Now a young man
was on the porch; he was leaning against the house and smoking.
He was maybe mid-twenties, loose dark hair, skinny. Good bone
structure. Olive skin. A little lost in his dress between adult and
teenager. Pants baggy but not too baggy, t-shirt somewhat sarcastic
in its depiction of stick figures with missing body parts.

I squinted up at him. "I was looking at the lawn."

He stared at me.

"I live down the street. Well, my parents do."

He nodded. "I'm Darrin," he was putting out his cigarette now,
"my parents live here."

"I used to know the guy who lived here pretty well."

"Cool," he nodded.

"Well, it was nice to meet you," I smiled the way my mother would—a safe, close-lipped departure smile—and began to back away toward the street.

"Well, hey do you want to see the house? My parents did a pretty crazy remodel."

I stared at him, scanning my body for any pain in the word *remodel*.

"I mean, they're not home, they're in Tucson for, like, a month. I'm just watching the place."

And I did want to see it, and I did want to stay out of my mother's kitchen for longer, so I followed Darrin through the front door, letting the smell of strangers and wood polish shroud me as the screen door slapped closed.

Mr. Blue had kept his house particularly neat, but it had always wanted for things like natural light. He had had grandmother taste, too. Mothy afghans, eyelet curtains, wood paneling. Now I followed Darrin through fresh rooms, walls painted the color of raw pasta with crisp hardwood floors and a new, open kitchen with black countertops that shone like oil. He narrated the tour, telling me what had been done; he even leaned down to finger some molding that he himself had helped with. "Yeah," he said, "my dad and I did a lot ourselves. He's a beast with woodwork. Hobby of his."

"Well, the place looks nice, thanks for letting me see it." We were in the kitchen and here again I employed my departure smile.

"No problem," Darrin shrugged. He really was beautiful.

"I spent a lot of time here when I was about your age."

"How old are you now?"

"Thirty-one."

"Huh."

"Yeah, it's kind of funny," I said, running my thumb along the counter edge, "I was in love with the man who lived here."

"With Mr. Blue or whatever?"

"Yeah, I really wanted him."

"That old guy?" Darrin stopped leaning against the counter and folded his arms, "You wanted to fuck him?"

"Yeah. But he wouldn't. The age difference bugged him."

"Huh. I don't know what's weirder, that you wanted to or that he wouldn't." At this point he was talking to my breasts so I didn't say anything else.

"Well," he fake-coughed. "Thanks for coming by." And he snapped the browned fingers of both of his hands before clapping them together, one curled in a fist, the other covering it. His own closing gesture.

"Do you want to see how I tried to seduce him? It's actually pretty funny now that I think about it."

"Umm, okay. Sure, I guess. I mean, if it's funny."

"Yeah so he was standing right about here." And I put my hand on Darrin's arm and guided him to just in front of the sink.

"I was thirsty, and he kept the glasses in this cupboard. So I just reached up, and . . ."

But this time it worked. When I gave Darrin's left earlobe a little suck I felt him sputter, he giggled before putting a hand immediately on my breast and turning his head to kiss me.

We kissed for a few minutes, hands under each other's shirts, when I heard a bird singing and told Darrin I had to go but would come back later.

"Why do you have to go?"

"Because it's my birthday." He stared at me. "My mom's cooking."

My mother's kitchen was full of men. My father had appeared, where he was now making everybody drinks from a recipe he had seen on TV, and my mother marveled aloud about how now the man had all the time in the world and what did he watch? The Food Network. My brother and his partner were there too, infusing the room with their charm, teasing us all. I took one of my father's new old-fashioneds in a sweaty glass and floated on its smoky warmth and the tomato air and even through dinner didn't mention the birds, or Darrin, or the other thing I'd intended to tell them. For dessert, my mother had made my favorite, chocolate Bundt cake, but she had only stabbed in three candles. For three decades, she said, and something about the three candles, two already listing over, like drunk wise men, made me want to cry. Though they were easy to blow out and the cake was black: spongy and perfect.

I was back over at Mr. Blue's at 1 a.m., wearing my pajamas, with a flashlight and slippers. Darrin laughed when he saw me. "You look like someone out of Nyquil commercial," he said. I looked at him with the flashlight under my chin and he grabbed me off his porch and pulled me on top of him right in the hallway.

I asked him, "Can we go outside, on the lawn?"

"What?"

"The lawn."

"What if someone saw us?"

"Who?"

"Anybody, are you crazy?"

So we fucked twice before dawn, but none of them outside like I'd fantasized. But it was okay, because I began to imagine that Mr. Blue was doing it with me in his old living room, and in his old kitchen, and I felt like his smell came back to the house, until the last time I came I was sure it was by the ghost of Mr. Blue, pouring his otherworldly regrets into me. In between, Darrin and I talked on a blanket on the living-room floor. It turned out he was a deejay, and was passionate about video art. He had not read *Walden*. Eventually he fell asleep and the way he breathed when he slept made him seem so much younger. I didn't sleep but stared at the ceiling, and the new walls, and the dark shapes of furniture, and they were like sleeping giants around me, and I felt so small, like Gulliver traveling the second time—a reference I knew Mr. Blue would appreciate. I let out a little "ha" at this thought, and when I heard my own small sound in the thick night, I realized his death was not a presence, nor a return, nor a ghost, nor an orgasm but only, really, finally, an absence.

I curled up against this, hiding under the sound of Darrin's invincible sleeping breath.

When early light came, the room turned purple almost instantly. The birds began to sing their recordings, and I knew it was time to sneak back down the street the way I had always planned. Not on the sidewalks, but through the backyards and across fences until I was at the house right across from mine, then a quick dart across the street. This was a plan so that Mr. Blue would never be implicated should someone see me. He told me he was sure I would be shot or arrested, snooping through yards like that. This was a conversation I'd imagined between us, but that had never happened.

I kissed sleeping Darrin, and told him I'd see him around, but he didn't wake up, so I padded out the back door without ceremony. The grass in the back was too messy, too wet to even think about Mr. Blue as I went over the first chain-link fence. It was more awkward than I had imagined, especially with the bubbled toes of my slippers too large to fit in the diamond spaces of the fence and in the end I caught my pajamas on the top and tore the right pant leg open. I decided to fuck it and take to the streets. I could always plead extreme sleepwalking, like those people that kill other people in their sleep.

I walked as quietly as possible along the fence I'd just jumped, toward the street until it turned into a hedge, and I had to crouch down, away from its upper branches. One branch caught my hair and as I turned to try to unsnag myself I heard a crunch. I thought for sure I'd stepped on a snail but as soon as I got my hair loose I cupped a hand over the flashlight, turned it on, and crouched down to see. It wasn't a snail.

In the dirt beneath the hedge lay the fragments of an egg. Blue cracks but no bird. The yolk stain gave the inside of the pieces a hopeful, if not disgusting, glaze. It looked like it had been the size of precisely nothing. Bigger than a fava bean, smaller than a Cadbury egg. But it looked familiar.

I picked up the three main pieces to try to reconstruct it but they flaked apart in my fingers. Still though, I knew the way I would describe it to my mother sometime later that morning. With a coffee spoon in hand, I'd say:

"It was like the size of the tumor they found in my right breast last month."

And then, with any luck, she would nod and ask me if I'd ever seen a bird egg before they went electric?

She would be willing to bet that I hadn't.

And it was true. I hadn't.

Dementia, 1692

We heard my mother scream just before daylight. The house was bathed in a blue presunlight and the color was the very sound of her wails. She had been trying to sit up with my younger sister but had fallen asleep and when she woke my sister was cold, her mouth open just a little, even the red of the rash gone white.

*   *   *

It was a year before that my sister and I had cracked open an egg on the scalloped side of a hand mirror. I cupped its two halves in my hands, pouring the yolk from one half shell to the other so that the white would drip heavily onto the glass. She held the pewter handle of the mirror and swirled the egg like batter on a griddle, the way Tatuba had taught us to do if we wanted to see our future.

Who will love us? We whispered to the glass and I crossed my fingers behind my back that in the eggy mirror would appear the face of John Tucker, the blacksmith's son. We waited, watching, heads together and I could feel my sister's breath on my arm. I saw our twisted mouths in the mirror and I giggled but just then Beth gasped and dropped the mirror, letting it fall where it landed face down but did not crack.

Skull! She palmed her cheeks, I saw a skull!

I rolled my eyes and picked up the mirror and wiped the soapy egg off with the frayed corner of my apron. The three-legged cat was already licking the floor clean.

Really! I did, I did! She grabbed onto my arm and I could see she really was afraid.

Ssshhh, I whispered, without tenderness, for it was too late, the tall Indian stood in the doorway. Tatuba looked at the mirror and the eggshell on the table, one half spilling yellow, and clicked her tongue. My sister ran to her and told her what she'd seen, crying now, saying that she would surely die. Tatuba held her to her skirts and said softly, Nah, some witch fooling you. But before taking her into the kitchen for some milk, she turned to me and scowled.

I stood alone and looked at the streaked mirror, its aging glass speckled black. I squinted hard but could see only my own pale face with its hook nose. My eyes the exact color of the mud that I had that morning scraped from my boot tread with a stick.

*   *   *

It started with a pink eye and a fever. Tatuba gave her root broth and sent her to bed. The next day she was no better and the third day she had the rash. The whole of her body was spotted red, like a pig's belly. My mother cried out when Tatuba asked her to come look and the doctor was sent for.

Dr. Phipps confirmed that it was measles and told us to wash her eyes and mouth with boiled water twice a day. I stayed in Tatuba's room. One night as she put me to sleep in her bed I asked her when Beth would get better. She stared at me for a moment and then took my sister's hairbrush from her apron pocket and pulled a nest of yellow hair from it. Using a strand of her own long black hair, she tied the nest into a small faceless doll, with only a head and a limbless body. Then she knelt and reached beneath her bed, pulling out a small wooden box. She took out a stub of a black candle and lit it on the lamp already burning on her small table. As she tilted the candle sideways, the black wax dripped slowly onto the doll, right where the heart would be. She chanted words from Barbados, the same words, over and over again like a song, quiet and fast.

When she was done, Tatuba blew out both candles and put the doll under the pillow we shared. I watched the wicks still smoking in the moon-filled room and wondered if a witch was watching us at that very moment. I snuggled closer to Tatuba's warm body but kept an eye open for signs in the darkness, waiting with both fear and desire.

*   *   *

A few months before my sister died, I did an evil thing. It was the neighbor's black-and-white dog, a mean and mangy mutt. One day, as I was waiting on the neighbor's porch for my mother to finish her visit, I told the dog, who was lying on the step, to get out of the way. Git, I said, and pointed, but the dog only looked at me and bared his broken teeth. So I gently nudged his flank with the toe of my boot, and he turned and bit me on the shin. It didn't break the skin, but tore my dress and left four teardrop bruises where his teeth had been.

I cried and my mother came out and scolded me. Don't you know anything? she said. Let sleeping dogs lie?

I wished that night with all my might, my hands squeezing together, that the dog would die.

Two weeks later, it was dead. Just like that. I thought it, and it happened.

I hadn't wished my sister dead, but I'd watched Tatuba make that doll and that dull black wax fall on her disembodied hair and I had thought, *that* won't help, and the next day she was gone. Besides, we'd looked into the future and had seen the skull. We had invited the death she saw then into our lives. The guilt of these memories was all I could think of, until even my grief became a shadow to it. I stayed awake at night, wondering if death would come for me, too. I broke the mirror with a rock, cracking it quick and quiet. I said it was an accident. And that I had accidentally cut myself. Even though it was really a sweet and welcome relief when I pried out a wedge of broken glass, cutting my fingers. The drops of blood falling to the fragments of my image in what I hoped would be both redemption and inoculation.

*   *   *

Years later I still think of that dog, and know it was not me that killed it, of course it wasn't, but still I am unable to divorce the memory of my throbbing bone with a raw and hungry guilt. It is as if my sister's death lives in the four pink imagined scars on my shin, and I can finger that smooth skin and feel over and over again that I did something wrong. That it should have been me.

*   *   *

Eventually I told my mother about the mirror and the doll and begged her not to tell Tatuba I had told her. I told her about the dog, too. She told me it was not my fault, any of it, and stroked my hair until I slept a child's sleep again. Still I longed to ask Tatuba if one always knew one was a witch, or if it could sneak up inside you, like a bad habit.

But there was no more talk of magic, white or black, until two years after my sister's death, when the neighbor's children became ill. The sickness started with seizures: strange jerky movements that seemed to rust their joints even while they were standing. They spoke nonsense. The youngest had been heard barking like a dog, even, and had red marks the size of a child's bite into an apple all over her little body.

The neighbor, Jane Good, was beside herself and came to my mother crying one afternoon. Tatuba was sweeping the kitchen and I was sitting in the corner sewing my first quilt. Mother sent me out to gather chicory, a fool's errand, but as I left I heard Mother Good say that her children were undoubtedly bewitched, and that her husband said he knew who had done it all right.

Widow Smithson lived on the edge of town, in a house half-fallen-down, with one side collapsed and broken so you could see clear through from front to back. The other side a tight little room just barely listing away from the collapsed side. She piled kindling, dead and crooked branches, everywhere in her yard. She fed all sorts of animals, so dogs, cats, and birds hung around the yard, too. She had no teeth and stringy gray hair and people said she drank. She traded with Indians, and sometimes had a bright red stone around her neck. There were hundreds of glass jars in her half-felled house, jars filled with the leaves of dried plants and animal hair and horns. For a fee, she would vanish your warts or heal your pox. She could also tell the future by reading your own hand like a book. Though now most people went to Dr. Phipps, especially after the new reverend called her work white magic and deemed it *of the Devil.*

I found a few stalks of chicory and, gathering the corn-blue flowers in my apron pocket, I headed back to the yard where I could see tall Tatuba, shaking out Pa's wet pants to hang. I watched her stern face as she clipped flapping legs to the line.

Come, help me, child, she said when she saw me. She handed me a damp blue dress of my own to hang and, as I did, she looked toward the kitchen door and then reached into her apron pocket and pulled out a small white nugget on a piece of twine. This, she told me, is a black rabbit's tooth. It's for protection. I want you to wear it under your dress, and then put it under your pillow at night. If that spirit's got them Good children, it might get hungry for you, too.

I put the tooth to my nose. It smelled like nothing, like snow. Tatuba tied it around my neck and I tucked the long nub under my dress just before Mother called to me.

The Good children became the talk of Salem. The following Sunday during sermon, Reverend Pratt asked us to pray for them. The three, all towheaded, were sitting in the front row. As he called on the Lord to help battle the Devil that besieged them, the youngest Good girl, the one that had the bite marks, a curly-haired cherub of a child, began howling out like a kicked dog. The whole congregation shifted and whispered, like restless water. Mother herself went flourwhite and grasped me to her hard. Still the child bayed. Reverend Pratt preached above the howls, yelling at us to pray that the Devil would let this child be. He grew more and more angry as he yelled at us and at the Devil. His tall, thin body paced and he preached and paced quicker and quicker, his spindly hands flying about him, and even from where I sat I could see the spit spraying from his mouth. As he smacked fist to palm again and again, I felt the little rabbit's tooth against my sternum, and rolled it across the bone under my dress. My mother and several other women were crying when Reverend Pratt finally stopped his sermon, took a bowl of holy water, and dumped it over the child's head.

The room went silent. The child was still and Reverend Pratt leaned over and stroked her wet hair. She seemed to see, then, that all gathered were looking at her and she started to cry. The congregation sat in still and silent awe.

They arrested Widow Smithson the next day.

*   *   *

I still remember the unearthly wails of that child. A meeting house, quiet and orderly, completely swallowed by that high and even sound. Indeed, as time passed, and all that was to happen happened, it seemed that all of us disappeared into the small black gaping hole in that child's angel face. We were not impervious. A girl's mouth. All it took. I think that and I feel that old fear. That old desire. Smoking wicks in the moony dark.

*   *   *

A few days later Mrs. Good came over in her work dress. I was out in the yard trying to get the three-legged cat out from under a cart when she came. Child, she said and hurried to me. Then she looked around before she reached into her apron and pulled out a jar of yellow water.

Child, give this to Tatuba, or your mother, and for the heaven's sake, do not open it and do not let anyone see. Not your pa, you hear?

I nodded and took the jar as she turned and walked quickly

away. I watched her body rock, her large bottom toddling as she disappeared down the road. Then I walked slowly to the kitchen door, examining the contents of the jar on the way, tipping it up and down to catch the sunlight.

I put it on the table with a smack so that Tatuba would look up from her darning. It's from Mrs. Good, I said.

Good Lord child, get that off the table, here give it to me.

I grabbed it and held it back for a minute.

What is it? I started to open the jar. Is it tinkle? I asked. It looks like tinkle.

Tatuba grabbed for the jar, but I was quicker. I put my hand on the lid, and started to twist it. I had to hold it carefully to keep any of the liquid from sloshing out while I grinned my threat at Tatuba's scowling face.

Tatuba signed and said, Child, that's for a witch cake, so don't you play.

I immediately put the jar in her hand. She knew she'd won with that one word, *witch*, and picked up the jar, turning away, taller.

I followed her and pulled her skirt a little. Tell me, I said, tell me.

She sighed and looked out the open kitchen door. When she spoke, it was a whisper. One can see if someone is bewitching another by making a witch cake. You make it from rye meal and the piss of one bewitched. This, she said, wrapping the jar in a cloth, is of the littlest Good girl.

But how do we know from the cake? I asked, too loud.

We don't know, *ssshh*. Tatuba put the jar in the bottom of an empty wash basin. We know when we feed the cake to a dog. You see a witch's invisible spirit, some of her venomous wisps, go into the body of the one she bewitches, and is even in that there, she said, pointing to the covered jar. Once we feed that cake to the dog, the witch will feel herself being chewed by a dog. The witch will scream in pain at the same time the dog is eating the cake.

So how will we know if Widow Smithson is screaming? She's in jail.

Your mother and Mrs. Good will feed the cake to one of the Good's dogs and at the same time I will go visit her in jail.

So you think she is the real witch?

I don't know, she said quietly. I don't think so, but that's why we make the cake. So we know.

*   *   *

Decades later, my mother's own widowed mind would flee. One of her last completely lucid nights, she would tell me that she had always blamed Tatuba for my sister's death. Not because of the mirror or the doll but because, did I not remember, Tatuba had been traveling the week before, to market in Boston to buy cloth for the Salem ladies. It was undoubtedly her that had brought the measles into the house. She would tell me, as firelight flickered against her open hands, that she had decided that it was God's will, then, that she condemn Tatuba.

*   *   *

The day the cake was baking, the house smelled like the woods in the summer heat when all the plants start to sweat their scents all over. They barely let it cool before they took the cake tin outside and set it on the back stoop next to a mangy gray dog that Mrs. Good had brought over. Tatuba had already gone into town and was, at high sun, supposed to be at the jail. I watched from the kitchen window as the dog ate the cake happily, pulling her lip up to show yellow teeth as she picked it apart. She licked the last crumbs and Mother and Mrs. Good looked satisfied, and they brought the tin inside and sat down and waited.

It turned out Widow Smithson did not cry out or scream in the jail and Tatuba was triumphant when she returned home. I said it, didn't I child? She patted my cheek. I said, No way is that harmless old lady a witch.

Mother suggested they write Reverend Pratt an anonymous note saying that he had perhaps arrested the wrong woman. But Tatuba thought telling him right out would be better. They spent the rest of the afternoon talking softly about who the real witch might be, Tatuba mending socks, Mother drinking tea.

Tatuba didn't come home the next day after market and Mother sat up all night, long after the last candle had burned to its nub. The next morning Pa took her to town to inquire, which is when Reverend Pratt somehow convinced Mother that Tatuba's cake was nothing more than a ruse, played on herself and Mrs. Good, in an attempt to free Widow Smithson, her sister in Devil-worship.

She would, he told her, be asked to testify at Tatuba's trial.

*   *   *

As her mind went, Mother's hair went from glossy black to stone gray within two months. She was no longer a woman, but a sick woman or, to the village children, a crazy woman, not unlike—I thought one morning as I walked her through town and saw two small girls pointing at her and whispering—not unlike Widow Smithson had seemed to me as a child.

When she still had some faculties, Mother told me she was cursed, that the witches had come for their revenge. When she lost her way home, she would tell the neighbors that a witch had put a spell on her path, moving familiar oaks and posts, to lead her astray. She would shake her head and cluck then, looking up to the cloudless sky in resignation to the Lord, or perhaps it was to Tatuba.

It seemed to comfort her, her imagined persecution, and was her one point of clarity for which I was grateful though I had never believed Tatuba a witch. Others, maybe, but not her, with her soft brown hands that were always gentle in my hair, and her pretty voice singing songs from church. But it didn't bother me to think of my mother's illness as Tatuba's revenge. It made me, in fact, a woman of thirty then, feel like I was a child again, listening carefully for Tatuba's footfall. Ready to tell her spirit that I understood, and would not betray her again. Ready, too, to ask her for mercy on my mother's behalf.

*   *   *

Summer swelled as the day of the trial came. Mother didn't want to go but Pa told her she would. He said if she did not, she would likely hang too.

I wasn't allowed to go, as children were not permitted, except in this case the Good children, and I was left to watch them disappear down the road in Pa's cart. As I waited for them to return, I went into the yard, to the edge of the woods and untied the rabbit's tooth from my neck. I took a stick and scraped a hole in the hard black dirt underneath a sycamore tree. I laid the rabbit's tooth in its shallow grave and whispered over it to protect Tatuba now. And Mother, I added, before folding the earth back over it.

When they came home Mother went straight to bed, so I had to wait for the next day to hear that she had told the court about the mirror, the doll, my sister's death. I screamed at her that she was a traitor and stomped outside, where I fell asleep crying under the sycamore tree, my body cradled over the buried tooth.

When I awoke I was empty, feeling as if my heart, too, had seeped underground. I had betrayed Tatuba once by telling Mother about the mirror and the doll, and now I had betrayed her again when Mother told the whole of the world.

*   *   *

Mother began to cackle and start at the very children that pointed at her. She did this, she said, because she was a witch. Did I not know? She started to drool, and to refuse her bath. Her hair become gnarled, her face sunken. Dr. Phipps, an old man himself now, gave me a sedative for the nights when she would rage and scream from the porch. Asking the sky to come and get her already.

*   *   *

I only saw Tatuba once more, the day she was hanged in the square. She looked taller and fiercer than ever on the scaffolding. The whole town was gathered. I watched her eyes, so white against her skin, and I both hoped she wouldn't look at me and hoped she would. Finally she did and gave me a sad smile. I thought I heard her say, Child, just as they kicked the stool she stood on, and there was a crack and a snap and then just the creak of the gallows' frame as she swung there. I saw her eyes stop seeing even though they were open and I felt like this was the skull my sister saw in the eggy mirror. Tatuba's. Her feet swung and I wanted to go to her, to hold her skirts and still them. I wanted her to shoo me off of her one more time, but Mother dragged me away.

*   *   *

Mother grew worse, unable in the end to even feed herself, before she finally died. One morning I went to wake her and she was cold, half of her face had gone slack in a way that reminded me of Widow Smithson's half-fallen house. I buried her next to my sister and Pa in the Salem cemetery, and as I began to grow old myself, my own dark hair streaking with gray, I wondered if my mind would go too.

*　　*　　*

Widow Smithson died in jail a few months after Tatuba's death, but nobody seemed to notice as Reverend Pratt had revealed that the Devil had indeed besieged us and witches were everywhere. I never went to another hanging, though there were several as I grew taller. I didn't live in fear of being bewitched, only the lingering fear that I was a witch. That Tatuba had somehow known this, which is why she had taught me some of her white magic, why she had looked at me with that sad smile as they kicked the stool out from under her bare feet. My suspicions were only made worse when Reverend Pratt published his pamphlet on the identification of witches. Among the numerous symptoms was a preternatural teat on the body, which is not sensitive to the touch. I had a mark just like that below my right hip, one that I could not feel, no matter how much I fingered it in my bed in the night. It made me sure I was not innocent, even as I knew I couldn't harm anyone—that I was untrained and impotent, protected still by Tatuba and the rabbit's tooth I had unburied after her death. I clung to its white dullness in the dark, feeling that old fear, that old shame, but no longer any desire, any curiosity to know magic.

*　　*　　*

In the end, it was my eyesight that failed me. Now, I fumble around the furniture, alone in my darkness, and hear the world outside edging around me. I feel them seeing me, a lonely old woman. Children throw stones at the house, the cracking sounds sharp and startling. After they are gone, I go out and feel for the stones around the side of the foundation and when I find them I bring them in and put them on my shelf. I roll them in my palms from time to time and try to guess their color. The youngest Good child, now an old woman herself, brings me a basket of food each week. She leaves it on the porch and does not knock and I let her think I can't hear her steps coming and going softly, though I would like to ask her about those days when she howled in the meeting house. I think of almost nothing but that time: of my sister's freckled face, of the mirror, the jar of yellow, Tatuba's hands, the dog eating the cake with greedy and indifferent judgment, and I think of Widow Smithson, dying alone in the gloom of the jail, and Mother, relieved even as her mind slipped away, and me, here in the dark, waiting. Waiting for Tatuba to come and pull my dress up, point at my unfeeling mark, my *witch's teat*, and shout to whomever will listen that I am not who I seem, and never have been, and I think this waiting, this, too, is punishment.

In July Flags Are Everywhere

*H*ow I grew up was, first, my grandparents went to war. When they went, my mom and dad and I stayed home and waited. In fact, I was waiting for a lot of things; I was waiting for the lifeguards at the local pool to notice me and waiting for my period to come and my breasts to come and this was so all-consuming that I never knew that all along I was waiting until the absolute hottest day in summer, when no one can even really move, for two young men to jog up to the front door.

The men were handsome and lately my grandparents hadn't been on my mind, not even my Nana, who'd sent me an ironed ten-dollar bill every birthday before she left. They had been gone two years and had become shadowy figures moving about behind my parents' lives. In the back row of the two annual Christmas photographs taken after they left, I could just make out the outline of where they should have stood, their glasses bouncing back the camera flash, their giddy figures hunched over the rest of the family.

The two men in uniforms came to tell us my grandparents had died, all of them in one to two weeks. They came to tell us on a July evening with the sprinklers going in the front yard; they jogged through a faint rainbow of airborne water to arrive at our door.

They carried a cooler and a bundle.

They rang the bell.

I answered. They were handsome. And important-looking in their uniforms. I called my mother, MAMA, I yelled, without looking away. I wished I had a cherry Popsicle. My mother came to the door behind me and she didn't think it was cute. She saw the cooler and the bundle and looked down like she'd taught me to do when I did something wrong.

Come in, she said.

Come in, I echoed. The pool out back was clean and I had visions of splashing their uniforms. Of them laughing. Of us all having a grand time.

She sat the men in the living room, and excused herself to get some tea. I wasn't going to follow her but she cleared her throat at me.

Out of sight, she outsourced: Pour some iced tea, she told me.

She called my father from the kitchen phone. I pushed two lumps of frozen ice into glasses and poured the day-old tea and went to get my new bikini on.

Come home, I heard her say.

A half hour later and two glasses of iced tea each, they told us.

All of them, within days.

My mother slumped from her chair to the floor and began to quietly moan. I noticed she had not brought out the coasters; the men's tea glasses were leaving water rings on the table. I went to the kitchen and got out two cardboard coasters with a hula dancer advertising a Tahitian beer; like the woman was the beer.

When I came back they had unfolded the bundle, an American flag bigger than our refrigerator door. One, the dark, handsomest one, held it tight through the center on one side. He asked me to hold the other side. I let the coasters drop and held the polyester flag while the other, the milky blond, took out a pair of florist scissors.

He cut it in perfect fours.

They laid the four pieces on the rug.

They opened the Styrofoam cooler.

They took out four pieces of wax-wrapped steak; it bled into the folds of the paper.

They put one steak on each quarter of flag.

The key turned, the alarm beeped, and my father was in the room.

The sight of the soldiers, or maybe it was the meat, brought him to his knees.

He looked at the men. Man to men. This exchange made Milky Blond bury his nose in his palm, almost protectively.

I'm sorry, he said, nose cupped. My father nodded, his face coiling up. He held his hands empty and open in front of him, palms suddenly big enough that in them I saw my grandparents one by one, like yearbook photos. They had done things. They had been there. There had been knitted scarves from one grandmother, cognac-soaked hankies from the other. Postcards from Florida. I, too, wanted to cry.

Might I say, handsome Dark Hair said turning to my mother, we know your parents fought with great valor.

My mother buried her head in his shoulder. I ignored a slight side cramp of jealousy.

And your father. Milky Blond spoke to my father. It was not his first tour. My father gave a teary nod. He was a true soldier; he and your mother both died heroes.

The whole country is indebted to your sacrifice, Dark Hair said, smoothing my mother's hair away from her hot teary face.

Milky Blond then pulled out a square of shiny white paper from his pocket. He unfolded it to show us a chart with two lines: one elevated and red, the other low and blue. This, he said, pointing to the red line, is the average courage of your parents. This, he said, pointing to the blue line, is the average courage of average Americans. It's much lower.

He paused for effect.

So, you can see how truly brave they were. Then he handed the chart to my father, who put his finger on the red line. His finger followed that line, shaking, and I could tell he was trying not to cry, faced with all of this statistical courage.

Milky Blond put a hand on his shoulder and I felt like the odd man out, my parents paired off with soldiers, the news so new it didn't feel real, only like the room and all the furniture was wrapped in Saran wrap, a clear but catching layer over everything.

They offered to play the piano for a while, but now my bikini felt like an old banana peel and my parents were both sobbing so I had to be the one to tell them to get out.

Get out, I said. But sweetly.

They left and it was still light. It wouldn't be dark for a while. This felt like an insult. I put a shift over my bikini and then slipped the bottoms off. My father had led my mother to bed, where I could hear her crying from down the hall, so I knew she wouldn't get after me for not wearing any underwear.

I carried the flagged meat bundle by bundle to the fridge. I had to clear space and throw out two cartons of strawberry yogurt, one expired, one new. I got the bundles in and went to get a sharpie to mark the date on them, but then I thought we'd probably remember the date.

My father watched me from the kitchen table, an untouched glass of Scotch before him.

The flag and the meat, it's a little political, don't you think? I asked him.

He looked at me but said nothing. This was to be the first of many times that he would go truck driving in his mind. He'd sit and stare for hours, seeing interstates and exits, though he was always only just in the house. I didn't know this then, I had to ask him a few days later and he told me that's what he saw when he went away without going anywhere. Even though he'd always been a CPA, never a truck driver. That first evening, I thought he was just in shock. I picked up his Scotch glass and he didn't flinch. I took a sip and coughed at the taste. Again he didn't move or look. I set it back down.

We could have drunk the whole glass this way. But instead I went to bed.

I didn't see my grandparents very often when they were alive. They hadn't lived close before they were drafted. We saw them on holidays, when they came to visit, and during the summer when we went to visit them in California and Montana. My father's father, Bubba, had been to war at least twice before; he was always volunteering, he always said he had to get out of the house before he died in it, which seemed now a misunderstanding on his part. My mother's father volunteered begrudgingly, abandoning their annual RV road trip in Keller, Texas. Better me than her, he'd said, patting my grandmother's bottom the last time we saw him. My grandmothers, I don't know. My parents didn't talk about it. I imagine they did not go happily. Although Nana had written that it was thrilling, and she was mostly doing camp work, keeping up morale. I always thought they'd come home because they always said that in the letters: Be Home Soon! Save some of your mother's pie for me! I hope you're standing up straight young lady or I'm going to give you a good whipping! That and they'd lived so long that all signs seemed to point to a continuation of that life. But then something went wrong and they weren't coming back and now I knew I probably wouldn't go to the public pool again for a while. At least not until my period came.

It turns out I had to stay home anyway because my mother became a child, and needed looking after, and so this was the second part of how I grew up. The morning after the soldiers came, my father got up to go to work and told me to look in on her in an hour. When I walked into their bedroom, shaded and dark, I saw her body had shrunk by about three times; just a tiny shape under the covers. Her eyes were big, too, and her hair matted down to her sticky face. Her vocabulary had turned child; she could mutter brief words but that was it.

No.

Yes.

Mama.

Water.

Dada.

She never said my name.

My father said it would take time. I should watch over her while he worked. He told me this when I was pouring grape juice over ice that night. His fatherness had gone so soft, like an apple sinking into itself, that I didn't have the heart to argue.

Over the next few days I did watch my mother and he did leave and go to work and come back like normal. I had no reason to believe he wasn't doing his job like nothing had happened. When he got home, he sat in the kitchen and drove his truck. I made us both sandwiches and my mother peanut butter and jelly with the crust cut off, which I found was the only thing I brought into her bedroom that she would eat. She would also drink a glass of milk with it.

A week after the soldiers came, I moved the meat to the freezer. Throwing out two freezer-burned tubs of mint-chip ice cream and a half-eaten loaf of bread to make room. There was no talk of my grandparents because there was no talk. My tan was getting dangerously light. It was still July.

Two weeks in, my mother got out of bed. Reduced and smelly, she dragged her body to the bathtub. Over the running water, she said she wanted to go somewhere.

Where? I asked.

The park, she said. And I saw in the clarity of her face that she was still a child and I would have to play with her. I hoped we wouldn't see anyone I knew.

At the park, it turned out she just wanted to swing. So I pushed her and she was quiet. She pointed to some ducks and I said, Yep, and then we walked home. On the walk home I noticed that there were still American flags everywhere, hanging from front porches, taped against the inside of front windows, staked in lawns. One with a yellow ribbon tied below it. I watched my mother to see if she'd notice and remember the steaks in the freezer, but she just walked with her head down, kicking a small stone before her every step.

She actually sat in the kitchen that night, while I made sandwiches.

What's with him? She asked me of my father.

He's driving a big rig, I said, It's Wednesday, so probably the Kearney to Chicago stretch.

Weird, she said, and giggled. I sighed as she dunked her sandwich in the milk and held it too long, so that the bread began to disintegrate into it.

Why don't you ever buy chocolate milk? she asked.

Outside the summer brightened on. The green was such it made your brain glow to look at it. One day I sat on the porch and watched the neighborhood kids build an obstacle course for their bikes at the end of the cul-de-sac. They were mostly younger than me but still it looked like fun. A few of them waved and one kid I used to babysit sometimes, who lived two doors down, rode his bike over to our lawn. He pushed his helmet up off his face and asked what I was doing.

Nothing, I said.

That's what I thought, he said.

I didn't say anything and he looked back toward the other kids.

Well, do you want to come play with us? You could be judge of who does the best trick, we built this course . . . , and here he pointed to the rubber cones at the end of the street.

I can't, I said.

Why not? he asked, picking his nose.

I looked back at the open front door.

He nodded, Oh, he said, You're grounded. He shrugged and rode off, See ya.

I could have gone over but I didn't because I wanted to be able to hear my mother. When my father did speak, he was still clear on one thing: Watch over her. I got up and walked to the street, and watched the kid go off the jump they'd made from plywood before I raised the rusty flag on our mailbox. It squeaked. I put it back down. Then I raised it one more time, hoping people passing by, or the postman at least, would read it as a sign saying both: "Leave Us Alone, For God's Sake We're Mourning!" and, also, "Help Us!"

The third week it finally happened. I went to the bathroom and noticed a brownish stain on my underwear. The next stain was a red butterfly. It was slow and light but it was there: I wanted to shout out loud, I felt such relief. I wasn't that far behind: I WAS

GROWN UP (this is the third part of how I grew up). I pulled up my pants and left the toilet unflushed while I went to get my mother, but when I jogged into her bedroom I saw her lying on her stomach on the rug, rolling bath pearls under her palm until they softened and squished. She looked at me curiously and I felt a little sick with panic. I didn't know what to do; didn't know the first thing. Should I wear something? Take an Advil? She looked up at me with big eyes and rolled a bath pearl over to my barefoot.

What? she said.

I looked from her to her bathroom, where I knew there must be answers, or at least maxi pads.

What? she asked again, flicking another pearl my way.

I watched the little pink sphere roll up to my big toe and stop. I wanted to squish it, and then squish all of them and then scream at my mother to come back to us and hear what I had to say. But instead I turned to go.

See you later alligator, my mother sang behind me.

I turned back around.

Where's your mother? I asked her and the words felt raw even in my mouth, like I'd been sucking on an ice cube.

I felt the chill spread through my whole body.

She stared back at me for a moment before looking down at the carpet, and now my face smoldered. I wanted to swear and I wanted to cry. I could see my Nana shaking her head at me as her daughter crawled over and picked up the bath pearls at my feet.

Mom . . . , I started, but stopped. The word didn't quite fit.

So I folded a paper towel in eighths and stuck it in my underwear before walking to the corner store to buy chocolate milk. On the walk back I ran into a boy from school; he didn't seem to notice the change. He just waved and said I looked pale. Get a tan! he yelled over his shoulder as he biked the other way.

The next day I really did lose it at my mother and I didn't feel bad about it. I woke up and was making a bowl of Grape-Nuts when I heard her giggle. She had been up early and turned the entire living room into some kind of fort. She had draped every quilt in the house over pieces of furniture, even turning the coffee table on its side.

I knelt down and peered in.

She was in the back corner of her fort drinking a Coke and eating stale fun-sized candy bars that must have been left over in some corner of the pantry from Halloween. A chunk of Snickers had melted into the carpet when she had accidently sat on it. She showed it to me and giggled.

You know what it looks like? She asked, covering her mouth in glee.

ENOUGH, I screamed, ENOUGH! GROW UP! GROW UP! And I tore at the quilts, like I was Godzilla, stomping and pawing at it until her fort collapsed on her. I pulled the quilts off of her and bared my teeth at her teary eyes as I tipped the coffee table upright. I slid the chaise lounge back in to place and pointed to my parents' room. She got up sulkily and slammed the door behind her.

I'M GOING TO GET A TAN! I screamed at the closed door and then I went to get a wet rag from the kitchen. I started to cry as I scrubbed at the chocolate stain. I scrubbed until the carpet was too wet to see if the stain was still there or gone and I didn't care. I gathered the quilts, ones my Nana had made, in my arms and took them into my room. I set the pile carefully on my bed, like a sleeping child, then I lay down and spooned the soft heap, pulling one over my legs even though I wasn't cold. I cried and fingered the stitching, following star patterns over and over again. I cried and cried, and thinking it must be hormones, I let myself cry more. I cried myself to sleep. I didn't dream and woke to my father standing over me.

You look more and more like your grandmother every day, he said.

Tomorrow I'm lying out by the pool, I said.

Okay, but check on your mother.

Last I checked, she can swim.

I raided my mother's bathroom cupboards the next morning while she was still asleep. I took four maxi pads and three tampons. And the folded directions from the tampon box. I read them in the basement bathroom, the most private room in the house. The tampons seemed complicated. So I went with a pad, easy enough, though it looked like I had a diaper on under my swimsuit bottoms and made a sound like a crêpe dress when I walked. I decided I just wouldn't get in the water.

I lay out until my back was the color of glazed turkey. The front of my body would have to wait for another day. My mother came out once and put her feet in the pool. I noticed she was getting taller. She was almost my height.

I'm bored, she said.

Oh, I said. Well, why don't you clean the house?

She stuck her tongue out at me.

All in all, it was a good day.

The fourth week marked the approach of the month anniversary since the soldiers had come to our house and I had plans. I called the local base and asked them to please send out the dark and light-haired soldiers.

Our boys are busy, said the man on the other end.

They promised to play the piano, I said.

They what? The man asked.

We lost all of my grandparents in the wars at once.

There was a pause.

I'll see what I can do, he said. And I'm sorry.

Tell them Wednesday at 6 p.m., I said and hung up.

That night I moved the steaks back into the fridge. I made spaghetti, which my mother would now eat. She slurped noodles while my father stared. I wanted to tell him the plan, but I wasn't sure he wouldn't suddenly father-up and stop it. So I asked him what he was doing Wednesday night.

He looked up to the left and said he thought for sure that he'd be somewhere between Reno and Cheyenne.

Tuesday I lay out again and tanned my front side. I didn't need the pad-diaper anymore since the blood had dried up for now. I hoped that by the time I needed it again my mother would be a mother again.

She came out midday in a swimsuit and lay out on the chair next to me. It was almost normal but I didn't dare say anything. I didn't want the spell to break. And it didn't, for twenty minutes, until I couldn't help myself from asking if she had sunscreen on.

Do you? she asked accusingly.

No, but I don't have your skin. You'll fry, I said, go get some on.

You're such a nag, she told me and turned over. I was turkey colored already, and so I thought I'd set an example.

I got up and put my cover-up on. Want to help me with something? I asked.

Fine, she said with a sing-song of annoyance that I knew she'd learned from me.

Inside, I opened the piano bench, which was stuffed full of old songbooks and music sheets. Tomorrow, I said, I am planning a surprise concert for you and your parents. Would you pick their favorite songs? You can make a list. Also, if you know any of dad's favorite old songs, write those down too.

I like surprises! she said and started to smile, then stopped herself. With a mock begrudge she muttered, Okay, I'll help, and she went to get a Coke and a notepad to make her list. When she put the Coke can on top of the piano, I refrained from repeating her own rule about food and drinks near the instrument, and instead just slipped a coaster underneath. A coaster with a cartoon dolphin. One Bubba had brought us from his first tour.

Wednesday morning came and I filled two glass pitchers with water and tea bags and put them in the sun outside. I swept the porch and cleaned the house for the first time in weeks. I got my mother on board by telling her it was for the surprise, and that some handsome strangers would be there. She agreed to wipe down the tables.

At four o'clock I took the meat out of the fridge. My mother leaned against the counter and watched me. She was my height now. I watched her eyes and hoped she would have some faint recognition. She did seem quieter.

What are you going to do with it? she asked.

I'm going to have Dad grill them up, I said.

But won't he be in Cheyenne? she asked.

No, he's coming back, I said. For the surprise.

I unwrapped each piece of meat and piled the flag pieces on the counter. They were brown and red with watered-down blood where the wax paper had leaked. I put the steaks on a large cutting board and went to the garage to get my Dad's hammer.

For one hour straight, I pounded on the purple and brown flesh, turning the steaks and flipping them until they turned the corner from tender to something else. Something more tenable.

At five o'clock I delayed the automatic sprinklers. I took a shower and then put on one of my mother's bras that had been left on top of the dryer for a month and found it wasn't so big for me after all. Next, I put on a white cotton dress that made my tan look even darker. I did my hair up and put on a bit of lipstick taken from my mother's purse in the hall. I snuck into her bathroom once more and squirted myself with perfume.

At five-thirty my father came home. The boss called, I told him, as he went to sit in his kitchen chair. Cheyenne cancelled. You're not needed tonight.

For a moment, my father's face looked like he'd been slapped. I held his arm and led him to the living room. But that's great, I said, you can serve drinks for our guests, and I need you to help me grill some steaks. He nodded.

At six o'clock the doorbell rang and there they were. I opened the door with great expectation, but they were somehow different. Maybe younger than I thought. Hello, they said.

You've grown up, the Milky Blond said as I ushered them in. He stared at my chest. Dark Hair scowled at him and then turned to me and said softly, Of course you have, with all you've been through.

I wanted to kiss him right there.

Hello there! A coy voice said behind me. I turned and watched in horror as my mother paraded out in my bikini. Her arms and legs were rose red from laying out, her stomach fish white. I put my hand over my eyes and took a deep breath. I am not going to react, I told myself and led the soldiers to the kitchen, and this was the fourth part of how I grew up, or at least when I stopped counting.

My father immediately went to work pouring out five glasses of sun tea. When my mother said she wanted Coke, he gave her a look and she went silent.

Milky Blond cleared his throat and I asked if we should eat first.

Grill's heating, my father said. I thought he might add on a ten-four but he didn't.

I pulled the steaks out of the fridge and suggested we all go out to the patio. Dark Hair paled a bit when he saw the pile of flag pieces on the counter.

He cleared his throat, You didn't have to invite us . . .

I gave him my sharpest look and his voice trailed off.

Over dinner my mother asked the soldiers question after question about themselves. I admit I listened when she asked if they were married? Girlfriends? Dark Hair was single. Milky Blond was engaged. His fiancée was in Topeka. They only got to be together every few months. My father asked them if they got out on the road much? I-80? I-9? I-40? He was baffled that they mostly stayed on base.

The meat was too tough, like chewing stale taffy. No one had the jaw strength to eat more than a few bites. It wasn't until the sun was low that my father asked, Now where did we get this? Wasn't it a gift?

The soldiers looked down like they'd done something wrong. I heard the sprinklers go on in the front.

How about some piano? I asked, and got up to clear the table. Dark Hair helped me. We let the meat slide heavily off the plates into the trash compacter. He said he was sorry it didn't come out better. He said he would talk to someone about that. I thought I'd fall in love if it weren't for all there was to be done.

We all went into the living room and I poured more tea. Careful to put coasters under everyone's glass. Tahiti for my mom, Hawaii for my dad. Souvenirs. I showed Milky Blond the list my mother had made, and we arranged the sheets and books so they'd be in the order of the list. He sat down and cleared his throat, shook out his fingers, and then laid his hands on the keys as if he was closing the eyes of the dead. He let them rest there for a moment before he jerked them up and began to play.

The first song was familiar, a ragtime tune that I could recognize but couldn't summon the words that moved silently on my father's lips. My mother was tapping her bare foot. The next song I knew was "The Very Thought of You," and the few that followed were upbeat and old time. Songs I had heard my whole life, during the holidays, when my grandparents were here. Dark Hair asked me if I wanted to dance, and I did. It was my first time dancing with a boy and he was being nice. I knew this, that he was being nice, that I was too young and too lanky. I stepped on his foot once but mostly did fine. My mother clapped excitedly. My father watched us move, and did not go driving. It was the liveliest evening we'd had in months, maybe even in years, maybe since my grandparents had been gone. We danced for three more songs, until I was almost out of breath but felt I was getting better. Dark Hair even said I was.

The last song we danced to was "Summertime," and it was slow and sultry, and I dared to put my head on Dark Hair's shoulder. It was not as comfortable as I thought it would be, but I let my cheek rest into his shoulder bone. He smelled a little like sawdust. Our bodies leaned closer to each other. When the song ended Milky Blond cleared his throat. Dark Hair stepped away, holding my hand still. Milky asked him to relieve him at the piano.

And that's when it happened.

The first song Dark Hair played was "Edelweiss." It was slower and it echoed against the walls like a drunk waltz looking for its way out of the hot room. My father's face began to look waterlogged with age and my mother put her face in her hands. This was it, this was the song that her mother had loved. The song that she loved. The third round of small and white, clean and bright, she looked down and seemed to notice her bare red thighs, her pale stomach. She put her hand to her mouth and disappeared down the hall.

When she returned she wore a flowered summer dress. I was sitting on the floor by the piano; "Somewhere over the Rainbow" was playing now and my father was quietly sobbing and Milky Blond had a hand on his shoulder. My mother came over and pulled me up to hug me. I saw that she was her normal size again. Slightly taller than me. She held me so tight it was hard not to start crying. I wanted to tell her right then and there about my period but I didn't want the men to hear.

She let go and went to my father, taking over for Milky. She held him and softly sang the lyrics his mother used to sing to him.

We all sat quietly as Dark Hair played one more song, a slow one I didn't know, my parents embracing each other. My mother motioned me over, and I crawled under my father's thick arm; it had grown heavier with all his driving. He held me tight and I buried my face in his father scent.

When the song ended, I met Dark Hair's beautiful dark eyes and he nodded and then he and Milky Blond quietly left us posed in this scene of grief, this surprise performance.

I watched through the window as they jogged through the sprinklers into the street.

The next morning, I got up early to do the dishes but found my father had done them before work. He'd left a note saying he'd be back to take us to a real steak dinner. I took the meat-stained flag pieces outside to the back patio and I lay them out by the pool, remaking the flag. I went in and got Scotch tape and began taping the pieces together but they had dried into stiff creases and wouldn't lie flat and I knew tape wouldn't really stick but I tried anyway. As I taped, I thought of the handwriting of each of my four grandparents. The boxes of cookies wrapped in foil, their voices too loud on the phone. Bubba saying he'd be all over something like a duck on a June bug. It was strange that all of that was not anywhere anymore, just gone.

My mother was in the kitchen when I went inside; she offered to make me a piece of toast. She said I ought to get out, enjoy the summer weather, and offered to drive me to the public pool. The lifeguards are cute over there, she winked. At first I just stared at her. But then I told her I'd rather go the mall. I needed some new underwear.

Later that evening I reset the sprinklers to turn on at their normal hour and remembered the flag I'd left on the patio. I hurried out back to get it, worried that one of my parents would see it and we'd be back to where we started. The flag was right where I had left it, but the pieces had been washed and sewn together. My mother sat in a patio chair with a vodka tonic, staring at it.

You got your period, she said, and nodded to the laundry basket at her feet.

I blushed and knelt down to finger the neatly stitched seam. My mother put down her drink and came over.

Help me fold it, she said.

And so we stood in the green glow of summer while the sprinklers went on out front and we folded the flag in halves, then fourths, then eighths, the flag growing smaller as we stepped together until I felt that we could keep folding and folding until the flag disappeared and it was only our four hands left coming closer together, making empty motions, one over the other, over the other.

Father/Writer

*H*e used to tell himself he was a writer of stamina. One that could really get at it, whatever it may be. Loss, for example. He'd gone inside underneath it, written it forward and backward, stories of amputees and widows alike. Likewise, pain. After a hiking trip through the Peruvian rainforest one summer, a blister had turned into a staph infection, a red deadly line from his foot to his heart. He'd been airlifted to the hospital in Lima where even then he told them: No, no painkillers por favor. He had a past. That's right, addiction—he'd been there, knew it, went up and over it and tried to write about it in a way that hadn't been done a million times before. Yes—a writer of breadth and depth, he used to think.

But then he had a child. Not just a child, but a daughter. And a daughter throws you and he was thrown. Not when she was coming, no not then, then he had been ordering pink onesies with literary-criticism jokes. But when she came, and he held her wet dark head in the palm of his hand, so tiny he could squeeze it, then he was thrown. Thrown by his sudden massive interest in another human. So different than the one he had in his wife. Thrown by this sudden and overwhelming urge, this need, to protect her—so much so he snapped at the nurse who leaned in to check her heartbeat. Gentle, he growled at her. So much so that he tried to describe it to his wife and found only cliché. That first night home, he took first shift and sat up staring at her, her face still swollen, her breaths coming like small and distant footsteps. He stared at her and only looked up to check the glass front door. Why was it glass? He wondered. Anyone could break it. And it was then in those first nights that he began to feel that with this overwhelming urge to protect was also an overwhelming sense of failure. It was already an impossible task, to keep her from the world. The things in the world.

And some of these things were bad, especially for daughters. And he knew that, knew because he had written about them. He wrote one story about a literary-minded serial killer who was obsessed with the reversal of time and who dressed the bodies of girls in period costumes. Some of his victims were only children. That was stupid, he told himself now, reckless, to write those things. To imagine twisted toddler limbs and to think there would be no consequence.

He held his child in the night, those first months, he fed her warm bottles, tipped just right to keep her from sucking air and watched her looking at him as she suckled, watched her hand, feeling in the dark, make its first reach to his face, and he told himself he wouldn't write like that, not any longer.

And it was hard, it was so hard. Making this adjustment. This life with child. His wife went back to work, and was always exhausted, and he stayed home with his child and tried to keep her safe as she grew. He still wrote, but he felt his own apathy. He'd made something so much better than anything he'd write. His agent called to tell him this latest manuscript, a story about a shipwreck he'd started just before his daughter's birth, seemed off. She sounded annoyed on the phone, and the baby was fussing. What do you mean he asked? Even though he knew. I don't know, she said, and he could hear her sucking air through her teeth. Watered down, maybe? He snorted at her pun and hung up the phone.

So he went from being an exclamation point to a question mark, and this is how he thought of himself, of his body, in bad similes. Even as he stooped to pick up his child, who'd become uncannily beautiful, who as she took from him, gained for herself, even as he did this he felt his failure.

He had dreams too. One in which a boy, with the face of a cousin's teenage son, appeared and asked to come with the family to a fair. In the dream, they were in a carnival crowd when their daughter disappeared, as did the dream version of the boy, and he ran everywhere to find them. Finally, on a snowy road he found her naked little body, pink as if from a bath, her torso cut open in an L shape. The boy nowhere.

He woke crying and gasping for air to his wife's sleepy look.

What? she asked him. What?

He could not draw out for her the space of fear his daughter had created in him. The shape of loss he was afraid may someday loom over him.

And so he stayed quiet when he could, but could not always or even often, and finally after his daughter's second birthday, his wife said, Enough, enough worrying and not writing and worrying. So he got a job teaching English at a high school.

But that was almost worse. There he heard the way boys talked about girls, the language they thought they'd invented but that he remembered well from his own adolescence, though he hadn't remembered the violence in these phrases, the objectification of hit that, or jackhammer. He felt as if he was surrounded by serial rapists, which made his wife and his agent laugh when he told them but they didn't see that it really bothered him. That when the boys slapped the girls' asses, or ogled their breasts, the girls giggled. Even the smart ones, the ones that surprised him in their midterm essays. And all this time, every day at 3 p.m., he would pick up his three-year-old at pre-K, and take her home for milk and pumpkin bread and read stories to her, and draw with her, and brush the tangles out of her hair, and wipe jam off her fingers, and sing to her at night. All this time, this little body still fell asleep on his wide chest, her breath deep now, her heart tapping against his own chest. Her weight still nothing. All this time, she slept on his chest and he felt as if his body was a boat surrounded by water and she couldn't swim.

But she grew, and more and more accumulated time in which he had kept her safe passed, and when she was four he started writing a science-fiction novel about a woman with extraterrestrial powers and his agent was thrilled. And the students had taught him about pop culture, about what sells, and he came back out the other side with a kindergartner, a three-book deal, and a career as a full-time writer.

The desire to protect, the certainty of failure, receded into the background, shrouded in a veil of monetary success, in a move to private school, in brand-new bike helmets, in a new gardening habit. Small successes frequent enough to ward off the disaster he had before been certain was waiting in the wings.

The next time the fear came back, it came to his wife, when their daughter was eleven. She hadn't been so worried when their child was young, or rather she worried about different things. Overheating bottles, rumors about autism and vaccinations, unvaccinated children, whether their daughter was growing too fast. She had never worried about the wolves in the night.

But then he came home from a Midwest book tour for the third book in the sci-fi series and found his wife tearing apart the house, throwing up cushions and opening drawers while his daughter was at soccer practice. What the hell, he asked?

She stopped and glared at him before tossing him a Seventeen magazine. Do you know she buys these? With her allowance? she asked. Did you? He shook his head and tossed it on the table, went to take a shower now that he knew the problem was hers. Later as his wife explained she had found one in her daughter's room, he tried to explain that likely it was fine, that those magazines were probably really for younger girls anyway, that that's the way the publishing world worked, especially for young adults. He gave her his most expert look.

She sat up in bed and looked at him incredulously. There was stuff in there about sex, she said. About birth control.

And he finally understood that this event had been precipitated by one two weeks earlier, before he'd left town. His skinny, dark-haired daughter had come home with an egg. She was tender as she set it on the red farm table in the kitchen and explained to her parents that this was her BABY for the next THREE DAYS. Her teacher had said that she had to carry it EVERYWHERE, feed it and put it in bed, and here she pulled out a cut-up egg carton padded with folded Kleenex tissue. IT MUST NOT BREAK, she said. His wife had looked at her with her head tilted, said how she didn't remember getting a letter home about this, and shouldn't there have been a letter? Steve? She had looked to him for help.

Do you have to refrigerate your baby? he had asked, and they'd both glared at him.

For the next three days, his wife had been on edge. She'd made constant comments about how real babies were a lot more work. You, for instance, she told their daughter, cried every day from 4 to 6 p.m., and did it again from 2 to 3 a.m. And the breastfeeding, good lord, the breastfeeding.

One night, as they got in bed, he had tried to tell her to back off, that their daughter was playing a fun game.

She was brushing her long auburn hair on the edge of the bed, a few strands in the back shown silver. He didn't know if his wife had noticed these. She plucked out the ones in front.

Remember, he said, taking off his glasses, when she used to feed and rock her baby doll, how she tried to potty-train it? I think that's more how she sees this. What he really meant, and probably should have said, is that his daughter was still all kid. She was small with freckles and even her teeth were still too big for her mouth.

God you are so naïve, his wife turned to him. The school will try and fail to teach them babies are a lot of work, and I asked yesterday when they are going to teach them about safe sex—it's not for three more years! That means we will have to do it, or else lock her up.

The thought of a conversation like that made him bristle. That was still a couple of years out, why was his wife trying to rush this growing up?

Relax, he said, turning over on his back, She doesn't even know any boys.

That we know of, his wife said. But one of the girls in her class has a boyfriend, she told me.

A boyfriend? He laughed, Really, who?

The Carter girl. His wife got in bed as he tried to remember who the Carter girl was, how she was different from his daughter. He knew she was different, but couldn't remember how.

But she's shy. It will be a while.

Are you kidding me? It's going to be here in no time. Boys, boyfriends, and hormones . . .

Listen, he said, as he turned off his light, No one is having sex around here.

Damn straight, his wife said. But as she turned off her light she chuckled, added: You walked into that one.

They lay in the dark joking about chastity belts, iron underwear, old guards of virginity.

A few days later, the assignment ended but his daughter hadn't wanted to throw the egg away. She put it in the fridge, and every morning for the next week he saw it when he went to get milk for his coffee. She had drawn a face on it, and glued a strand of yellow yarn to the top, complete with a drawn-on pink bow. Its name was Genevieve, he had learned, and he still did not feel the same fear his wife did. Everything about the egg, its hair, its fairy-tale name, told him his daughter was still his baby.

And so he said, Good morning, Genevieve, and hoped she wouldn't crack, or if she did, that it wouldn't be his fault.

And it hadn't been. It was his wife who knocked it off the shelf, making room for a bowl of washed strawberries. He'd never seen her look so content, wiping yoke from the tiles.

But that had been just the beginning of his wife's own watchfulness. She stayed up waiting for their daughter every night she was out over her teen years. He would try to get her into bed, and when that failed, try to joke with her again, calling her "ye old protector of virginity" even as they knew, had whispered, that she probably was sexually active. At fifteen she'd asked for birth control to help with menstrual cramps, a real suggestion by her doctor, but they knew she was serious with her boyfriend. That the cramps were likely an excuse.

It's the creeps I'm worried about, his wife said one night as she got into bed furious after their daughter had been fifteen minutes late for curfew. The killers. The rapists.

Do you know the statistical likelihood of something like that? He rolled over to face her, he had been half-asleep when she came in.

But that doesn't matter if that statistical anomaly is your kid, think of those poor parents last year . . .

I know, I know. He didn't want to think about it but he did. A girl in the next state over was picked up from school by someone claiming to be her mother's coworker. They found her body, mutilated, three days later. He hoped his wife hadn't reminded their daughter of it, too. Hoped she hadn't threatened her with imagined violence for being a little late. He could hear the sink in his daughter's bathroom down the hall. She was probably brushing her teeth, wiping off her makeup. He thought about getting up to go and kiss her goodnight. Thought about the way she'd roll her eyes at him.

I'm just saying, the shit people do. The monsters out there . . . His wife was whispering now.

He thought of his own old stories, the ones his wife, when they were dating, had told him were grotesque and creepy, the child bodies in renaissance wear. But he didn't mention them. Instead he told her, You watch too many crime shows. Not even the FBI has to deal with a serial killer every week.

I know, I know, his wife sighed. And the victims are always teenage girls.

He was tired. He rolled over, away from his wife's pink lamplight.

Besides, his wife added, she's beautiful.

He rubbed his eyes and looked at the lamp reflecting in the glass of the bedroom window, the darkness beyond, and briefly glimpsed that shadow from so many years before.

I mean, she added, drop-dead . . .

Okay, enough, he said, we've taught her to be smart about

things and that's all we can do. He said this but really he was still thinking he might get up, go tuck his daughter in, when he heard her bedroom door shut.

I guess. She yawned and turned off the lamp, but he was fully awake now and stared for a long time at the darkened window.

The next week he signed up his daughter and wife for a day-long Saturday seminar in self-defense. They came back and both started karate chopping his arms, his chest, and making fun of the teacher. A German woman who sounded a little too easy to make fun of, he pointed out. But really, he was jealous of the way for the next several days one of them would say JAAA, and the other one would crack up.

Still though, it was a good choice. His wife lightened up and so did he. He felt they'd done their jobs right. Raised a smart kid, kept her safe. Their house was busy, and warm. He wrote short stories again, and his daughter grew interested enough to read his drafts for him. She was a brutally honest critic, and he told her she had a good eye. She did.

And the years stacked up sloppily for him. Like teacups in their kitchen cupboard.

Then one day, when she was seventeen, he was out in the front yard weeding and pruning a rose bed they'd put in the summer before. The buds were still tightly shut and they reminded him of small scrolls waiting to unfurl their message. He thought about writing that down in his next book, he was back to literary fiction. He was in the corner of the yard, on the side of the house, when he heard a car pull up. He peeked his head around the house, out of the shade, and saw a white jeep he didn't know. He frowned and watched his daughter get out of the back seat. She wore all black and was tall and he watched as she slung her backpack over her shoulder and shouted thanks to the driver. She turned to face him.

Hey Dad! Roses, again? She squinted in the bright day and smiled at him, a brilliant, movie-star smile, before she strode into the house. He watched, dazed, as a folded piece of paper fell from the outer pocket of her bag as she climbed the front steps.

He stared into the empty daylight and felt those old waves again, a flare of anger, like he was being woken from a dream. First, he directed it at the strange car backing out of his driveway, the friendly goodbye honk. He fumbled with his gardening shears, letting them drop to his side. Maybe it was the way she'd said, Roses again? Like he was an old man.

The sun seemed bright, sharp, though the long straight shadow of the house fell over him. No, it was the car, revving too hard now as it drove away. But it was nothing this car, a friend from her drama group probably. It was nothing but his gut was knotted. A gut feeling. It was as if, he thought, he had not kept her from the wolves, after all. He had failed all over again. That Jeep driver could have been anyone. He wanted to march in the house and demand from his daughter, Who drove you home?

He remembered the darkness beyond the warm walls of their house all those nights.

That white jeep.

This woman in black. That smile.

He blinked and squeezed the top of his nose, letting out a sigh. It was a hot day. His gaze rested on the white square of paper and he walked over and picked it off the stone step and held it in his hands for a moment. He could see the ink veining through, could see it was a drawing. Not a note, so he could look.

He unfolded the picture. He recognized his daughter's style of drawing faces like perfect teardrops with curlicues and Charlie Brown jags for hair. The scene was intricate. A man. Clothed. A woman, kneeling, naked. Lactating or bleeding, or crying, maybe, from her breasts. Her throat cut in a dripping smile but her face very much alive. The man smiling. The woman screaming. The ink a thick black in the egg shape of her mouth. There was something oddly familiar about the picture. He felt that yellowed feel, that déjà vu.

He folded the page back up and slipped it into his pocket.

He retreated to the roses and stared at them again, remembering how they had already bloomed. Last year. He picked up the shears. Roses again. It would be dark within the hour. The yard was large and wooded behind him. He looked around. Tilted his ear up. Anyone watching him would have thought he had heard something behind him.

Had he? A rustling?

He remembered how just last year he had taught her to whittle branches from those woods, then, that same summer, to Rollerblade. But then that couldn't have been last year. Her Rollerblades were moldy in the garage, he'd seen them earlier when he picked up the shears in his hand. The egg child, he realized, was years ago now, a third of her life had gone by since then.

A rustling. He wondered vaguely if he should walk his property line.

That picture. It was the expression on the man's face. The desire, the pleasure. It was familiar. Those old stories he had written, could she have read them? No, they were long gone. He remembered how he had hated them after a while, hated the arrogance, the places within they represented. Crevices of animal. What he saw in them that maybe no one else did. Now though, he wondered, if maybe his daughter would see it.

Again, a noise behind him. Probably just a deer. But what if it wasn't? Who had driven that Jeep?

The evening sunlight rounded the house's corner in a sharp line, and this time he let slip the shears. He fell to his knees in the grass and let a dewy ache settle on him. His heart hurt a hot, tired hurt. A window was open and he heard his daughter laugh, his wife's voice.

Maybe he needed water.

He let his eyes close. He remembered everything now with a sudden violence: her tiny sticky fingers, her saying over and over, Dada, carrying her into bed after she'd fallen asleep in the car, playing peekaboo, playing hide and go seek, playing go fish, learning to braid her hair, the strands silky and weightless in his big fingers.

He looked down now at the clenched little roses and felt so useless, so lame.

He stayed on his knees until the sun had weakened into a faint pink hue. A dreamy glint that he tried to let remind him of how intact the world was at this very moment. An uncut peach, he thought, though he wouldn't write that down. And he was glad he hadn't marched in, asked his daughter who drove her home. Glad he hadn't insisted he'd heard someone in the woods. Even if he had.

Now he rose slowly from cold grass-pressed knees and went back into the garage to hang the shears, before going back in the house where the kitchen light was now on, bright and beckoning. He went in the back door, into the warm and familiar smell. His wife's voice as she talked on the phone, his daughter's TV show muffled. His latest manuscript spread on the dining-room table. Water boiling in the kettle. He went in and as he closed the door behind him he paused and, in a tired and useless motion, locked the door against the now brilliant red sky.

Warning Signs

*I*f I knew why my little brother shot himself through the head then, man, I'd be rich. Really, I would. Not just because it was the most irrational suicide known to mankind, I mean just look at what he was: Super good looking, the crème of the ninth-grade crop, blue eyes, sandy hair, olive skin, smooth jawline, well built; Super sporty, kid was the captain of the JV soccer and basketball teams and was already playing varsity in both; Super cute girlfriend, big doe eyes, long tan legs, perky sweaters; He pulled good grades, charmed the teachers, our parents would leave teacher conferences beaming, literally shining with pride at what they had managed to produce in him—such a relief after the girl, the gangly shy girl who was intelligent but who always gave rise to concerns from all facets of the community. So all these things he had as well as, apparently, the ability to blow his own head off, something that also—which I never realized until I saw his room afterward, and the splattered design of maximum chaos—took a special person. The kind of person that not only is okay with dying at the age of fifteen when your whole life appears to be awesome, but actively pursues it, and then decides that his head really is the problem and that if he's gonna go, man, is it gonna go and really all those thoughts you had seconds before are now dispersed in their most concrete, solid gray matter all over the fucking wall.

Not to be gruesome.

And all this is not why I'd be rich. Let's get back to that; I'd be rich because if I could figure out the *why* behind the deed I could get myself hired out to everyone with a teenage son because this shit is on the rise. All over the place, wrist-slitting, pill-taking, hanging, plastic bags over heads, hoses from car pipes, you name it, but the midpubescent boys in our town are dying fast and there isn't even a draft on. I could tell the town's worried parents that they needed to stop playing the Cowboy Junkies, or start feeding their kids an all-vegetable diet with limited sides of pig fat. That they needed to talk to their kid with pillowcases over their heads with smiles drawn on in fabric marker, AND that maybe this could all be done before their kid was dead and it was their fault, forever, if not in reality, then in some deep pocket of all their future days.

But I haven't cracked the case yet.

I'm still just stuck as the unfruitful, albeit disappointing survivor; although I have come to know several theories, many of them the by-product of my recently developed habit of hanging out with the regulars at Big MacDaddy's on Tuesday nights when shots are two-for-one. I start with some Stoli, then move on to Jack, and after that the whole bar's on Cuervo. That's when my grief becomes public, and we sit around and headshake, and sometimes Trudy Lee or Big Joe will sling an arm around me while we talk about what it was that kid started.

Theory One: That my brother was part of some underground cult born in the wet dream halls of junior high, a sect whose cultish quirks included a suicide pact. He, who may or may not have been the leader (see theory 1A, still to be worked up), was the first to cross over, and so they all slowly started to go, bound by their boyish, testosterone-heavy blood. Like leaves in the fall, there's always that first one to turn and the rest see it and man do things start changing. I list this theory first because it is immensely popular at Big MacDaddy's and in fact was suggested by the bartender, Trudy Lee.

Theory Two: That there's something they've all been taking, an over-the-counter drug, a protein powder or a muscle enhancer, some sort of penis growth pill, something that has a side effect of one day suddenly, compulsively killing one's self. Something that literally makes you leave a room full of high-fiving, laughing beautiful youth and go out to your car and electrocute yourself with your jumper cables, like in the case of Bobby Anderson. Who, by the way, was the JV quarterback—a beautiful boy who may or may not have been heterosexual (and this of course complicates his inclusion solidly in any theory as we live in a fucking bigot town).

Theory Three: That the boys were all involved in some murder and that the guilt was slowly eating away at their collective soul. This is a weak one, defended really only by Mel, the vet with one leg who is a Tuesday fixture. He does not seem to care that there really haven't been any unsolved murders in the past few years, just your average spousalcide, nor does he mind that not all these boys were close or ran in the same social circle, and perhaps didn't even know each other. (Also a noted problem with Theory One, though the cult would have been secret thereby deceiving us on the subject of their knowledge of one another, explains Trudy Lee).

Yet Mel insists that a body will be a found, someone no one would have missed, a faceless old woman living alone, perhaps. Or a runaway kid who nobody bothered looking for. Mel could even picture the murder he said, could dream of the bloody letter jackets.

But I am, as of now, unattached to any of these theories.

Partly because none of them explain this conversation I had

with my brother the day before he died. His eyes were a real opaque color of blue that day, like beach glass, and he hadn't washed his hair (there you see it now, don't you, a warning sign, but he didn't wash his hair lots of days, so go fuck yourself). He came and stood in the doorway of my room, staring for a minute at the terrarium where my corn snake Jerry lived.

Do you ever think about freeing Jerry? he asked.

Nah, not really.

You should.

Free him? But where would he go?

No, I mean you should think about it.

Well, yeah, I am mean, duh, yes, I've thought about it. Him escaping, and dying of starvation with no one to feed him frozen mice. It's not a pretty thought.

He'd be fine.

Yeah I'm sure he'd get a job, eventually save enough to go to college or get a degree in IT and write us from Silicon Valley.

You know, you can be an asshole.

Dude, little buddy, do you really want me to free Jerry? Is that what you think is best here?

I just want you not to be so fucking sure you're always right.

I'm not!

At this point in the conversation I closed the door in his face so I could get back to my online chat with CUZ1200. And no, I am not so brainwashed with grief that I really think Jerry was a metaphor here for my brother or anything like that. But it's this, see, he'd never known Jerry's name. Or he always pretended not to know, to forget, he almost always called him Snake or Snaky or That Vile Thing. So why did he know then? So why did he, on the downy eve of his death, finally call Snake by his name?

Now that's a warning sign.

But I didn't see it, nobody did. He came home from football practice, hung his pads up, threw his clothes down the laundry chute even though he was headed right down to the basement anyway, where my parents had moved his room after he complained he never got any privacy. His door shut and the stereo pumped on and we were all in our correct places; the ones we always inhabited in that hour before dinner: my mom was leaning over a cooking magazine in the kitchen with a paring knife in hand; my father had a bottle of beer raised halfway to his mouth out in the yard, looking over the baby spruce he'd planted a month ago; I was in my room checking out sales online, cursor hovering over tiny images of sweaters.

And we were all frozen like this, in our places, when he left his room and went across the basement rec room to the storage room and got my dad's rifle from the one year he thought he'd take up hunting but then discovered none of his friends hunted and he was a bad shot, and then he went back into his room, closed the door, restarted the song he'd been listening to and then, and then, he stopped time.

Just like that.

Which is when we all unfroze, came to motion. It was a loud sound and there we all were at the top of the stairs. Damn, a pipe musta gone, my father muttered and headed down first. My mother looked at me and we waited to hear my father curse the malfunctioning in the underbelly of the house. But instead we heard him call my brother's name, his music get louder as my brother's door opened, and then we only heard music.

We only heard music and no voices until my mother went downstairs and screamed and that's when my father turned off the music and I started down but he blocked me at the bottom of the stairs so I just looked over his shoulder at my mother in the hall and her bloody hands and her melting face and I felt the sudden absence in the house. It was a little like when the power goes out in the day and it's still light but it's different. A buzz was gone, a humming had vanished. The motor of this house, this whole family, the thing that kept us moving along with the rest of the earth had stopped and now we hung in space for I don't know how long before the funeral home and the police and the neighbors were there, buzzing us along again.

We just hung there.

I saw his blood, on my mother, on the wall, on seven loads of laundry, but I never saw him. Not like that. At the funeral home, I saw a corpse impersonating him but it was a pretty shoddy job since his head was covered with a paisley sheet. After the funeral, I dropped out of community college, I gave Jerry to an elementary-school science teacher I met at the bar cause he thought it'd be great to have a classroom pet; the boys would finally open up to him then. And I began my extensive work on wondering why, which first took me to Big MacDaddy's more often than not, and then it led me to start sleeping around, and then to start reading.

Proverbs, mostly.

Chinese, medieval, African, you name it, if the county library had it, then I checked it out. This was a result of another remembered conversation with my brother that hit me like a bus one day when I was walking to the IHOP to get some coffee since my mother had quit making it on any kind of consistent basis. It was a conversation we'd had a couple of weeks before he died, when I picked him up at his girlfriend's house and he looked a little flushed as he got in the car.

After a few minutes of driving I lit a cigarette and asked him if he and his girlfriend were doing it yet.

He was quiet for a few beats then he muttered, "Curiosity killed the cat," but he was blushing and smiling all shyly, so I laughed and arm-punched him.

"Yeah, but cats have nine lives, lover boy."

"That's good, cause you're going to need them all to learn how not to be so nosy."

"Oh come on now, How's it feel to be a man?" I said, using my best man-voice.

"Jesus, you're unbelievable."

"Well, you better be using protection . . ."

"Okay, Mom," and he rolled his eyes, "and you better watch it with those cigarettes or you'll get caught red-handed," he coughed dramatically and unrolled his window. "Seriously, she's going to smell it on you and kick you out. Plus those things will kill you."

"Okay, Dad."

"It's your funeral."

"Well, I hope you don't wear that shirt." He was wearing a maroon Harvard shirt our cousin had sent for Christmas and he looked down at it for a minute and then asked what was wrong with it and I told him he didn't go to Harvard and our cousin that did was an a-hole that's what's wrong with it and our banter continued unimportantly like this until we stopped and bought a few groceries for my mom, and a couple of candy bars which we ate as quickly as possible so they'd be gone by the time we drove that last five blocks home.

This whole thing was something I never would have remembered except for his putting a gun to his head and now I remember everything I can about what he and I said, reenacting the words and gestures on the walk to the IHOP and obsessing over what by now I am sure you've noticed: the kid used not one, not two, but three fucking idioms, clichés, old wives' words, whatever you want to call them, in that conversation—all of which might explain, or sure as hell describe, his death.

I don't need to break that down for you.

So now I'm wearing his Harvard shirt all the time and reading proverbs and thinking about my brother's lily-sunk coffin and the stupid dress I wore and my mother's red hands in the basement hall and her standing there holding them out and screaming like she's in a slasher movie and I'm wondering what it's like to die/ what it feels like/if he was afraid/if there's a suspension of all time as it becomes too late to take your finger away from the trigger/if my father will ever stop telling people that it was an accident, that my brother was playing with his gun/if it will ever get better now that there's a before and after and the former is a locked door, a terrarium of time that we can look into but cannot touch or hear or even smell.

I do all of this wondering and wonder most of all why the curiosity hasn't killed me yet, but maintain that

I'm on thin ice

Up shit creek

My chips are down, I'm under the weather, screaming bloody murder and waiting for you, Brother, to come, let the cat out of the bag/pick over my bones/make a clean sweep and don't

leave me out in the cold.

American Family Portrait, Clockwise from Upper Right

Prefather

The farmer went outside at dusk and the flies were working corn. He thought he was dead so he went to a fly combing soil, working seed between two legs, rubbing. He asked and the fly led him to a part of his land he could not place. It buzzed and he saw. It was a foot sticking out of the soil. And black as it was, it must have been the one that went missing some two hundred years ago.

So he wasn't dead.

(A photographic smudge, or perhaps his ghost, haunts the upper left of the portrait. Simmering in the black-marble backdrop.)

After All, or A Father

He tells us: Coal tear of the dough eye said uh-uh. And the rest of us, all cotton and wool in vision and pain, listened hard. But no one in pain can listen so we kneaded words and ate them so as to nourish our felt stomachs with the black of sounds we never understood.

He tells us.

(A smile on a face like his looks like a scar. A wounded effort at representing himself. His self a long, slow gasp for air.)

Devil You Know, or Mother

Blond fuzz, small sharp teeth, inhabiting the brightest aisles, hand on hip, chatting up colors and name brands. She moves the wheels, back and forth, pulling space in relation as you careen in the small metal basket. She makes sure that no matter what, when you reach out, you won't touch upon a name.

(Just perfect. Hair a golden cloud, the head tilt of love. Hands clasping others' shoulders in bony devotion. Though so much has slipped through those fingers.)

Oh Please, or Sister

Picture sister's skeleton. She looks like other gendered remains, hollowed beauty, amazing absence. Picture also, her skeletal coyote, a small husking thing. Picture her bones on all fours and her skull rubbing against her coyote's skull, in affection of course, both pelvises are up, all happy bone scraped dry. With only one tail, it's really a riot.

(Center stage with a bow, she rebels in little cuts all across her life. Places where the air gets in, the *her* gets out. All hidden by a peach blouse.)

As If There Were, or Brother

As if there ever was, even when named the thing like this in the back of your head in pushchair dusks, vomitous earlyday horizons and the rest of steroided time; it is always something else. Some other murdered little thing.

(Not pictured here.)

Daffy, the Third

Like the two retrievers before her, she sits straight, ears forward and folded, her breeding cascading down her fur, she is the sign. The sign of making it. The one that gets to be in the photo: the others, the glass Tupperware, the good parking space, the jet ski, have to be inferred by the arc of her tailbone, her manicured gait, her shine. Oh, her shine.

    (It's too bad her tongue hangs out in the picture.)

Other

(or Me, or You. Pictured as you are when you look in the mirror before a Christmas Party you don't want to go to.)

    They reached in, with delicate instruments, down into my mouth. Past even the tongue roots, they reached in, scraping mothertissue to find out if the walls were indeed alive. They reveled in the automatic nervous system's gentle sensuality, filling luscious voids with their invented armflesh. They reached in, one at a time, or all at once, and took them all. Jewels from under the me, red clots and black coal-like lists of facts, of certainty.

So we'll never know exactly what will kill us.

A mercy, maybe.

The Crossword

Across

1 A little lie
Like a white lie? Like a fib? Like something dead.
The old woman remembers now.
"Sometimes it's okay to lie, you know, like a white lie, or a dead-dog lie." Her father stood bent over the workbench, cranking a screwdriver.

"What's a dead-dog lie? Well, before you born, we had a dog, a damn good dog, best dog I ever owned, a chocolate bird dog named Wolf. Your mother and I took that dog everywhere, and for a long time it was just the three of us, especially after we lost that first," her father paused and wiped his jaw with his sleeve. "Well, it was especially the three of us."

Her father cranked the screwdriver harder before stepping back, away from the bench. He was making a bed, and she could smell fresh sawdust.

"One summer I was out in the oil fields, and one day while I was gone, your mother found Wolf dead as anything on the front porch. Now I've always thought that *s-o-b* Mitchell down the road baited Wolf with some kind of poison. See Wolf was always killing his hens, so I think that bastard killed Wolf. Wouldn't ever tell it though. Anyway, your mother knew it would break my heart, and she didn't want me out on the rig with a broken heart, so when I called from a pay phone in Galveston and said, "How's Wolf?" she said, "Oh he's fine, just fine."

"Now that was a lie, but it was for my own sake. So dead-dog lies, they're a kind that's alright, because really the truth is just hiding for a while till it can do more good than bad."

The pencil scratches over all the lines twice. F I B

Across

1 A little lie
4 Slapstick weapon
If 4 Down is right, if Ghost is PHANTOM, then it has to start with a P. It would have to be Pie.
That thing she hasn't made in years. Now the old woman eats only the gelatinous lemon kind that come in boxes with plastic windows. Her niece brings them to her. The kind that stick everywhere in your mouth. But she remembers the other kind, the made kind.

(She leans over the empty shell, furiously pinching the damp crusts between the knuckle of her index finger and her thumb. She usually likes this, but not today. She had wanted to be tender, to show the other girl, her cousin, what their grandmother had shown her, how to make a perfect edge to frame the smooth center (the dough should never be too thin or it will burn). But today the dough smells like a wet magazine. Today her cousin—standing taller, so thin she has a vacant look like she was a wire hanger for her own clothes—bothers her. She can smell the cigarette smoke in her cousin's hair.)

Down

16 City in Mexico

She remembered Guadalajara, "Do you remember Guadalajara?" she says out loud. The kitchen yawns back. All the mariachi, and the flowers in the market, and oh, do you remember the thunderstorm sky above the gold steeple in El Centro? She has another warm, vague notion. The kitchen opens its yellow eyes.

(One day she leans down to pet a dirty sleeping dog before she realizes it is really a dirty dead dog, lying in a dirty street.)

She pencils it in quickly. G U A river D A of L A stones. J A R A

19, 19 Across is Intoxicated like drunk, or happy, or consumed. There are five letters.

There were times when she had wished her life had been a movie, the old woman thinks, because then there would have been exact measures of gestures and words, and in the end there would have been some balance. Everyone that had gotten too mean would have repented in equal measure, or at least learned how to love without so many rules. She has always felt this way, since she was young, when she lived in other places. Not Idaho.

Well, it must be drunk. The old woman pencils in D

R

Those were times when her life was like a movie: when she sat, drunk, in the bathtub looking at her nipples and thinking that the bathroom and her body and everything, really, had a shiny veneered look.

U

Once, she was little, and he was big and smelled like hot metal, he told her she had stolen the little tin box of candies. I did not, I did not, she gave them to me, you were there, she gave them to me, remember remember remember. He looked like he was going to push, or hug too hard, but he just stumbled and the hard, pink candies bounced off the wood floor. He laughed like rain on a car roof while salt drew lines on the back of her throat. (If this is a movie, in the next scene she will run away on a train in a dress to a city and a job and a fast-paced life of wisecracks, and loneliness will only last three and a half minutes of staring out the new alley-facing window petting her new cat and glancing sideways at a framed picture with a little crack in the glass, of Her and her and him and even HIM. This picture will be all she has left of her old life, because it is just a memory, and memories are not even real living things but only thoughts you don't even have to have.)

N

(In the bathtub, the glass sweats. The ice tastes hot.) You never remembered the lime.

K

You just stooped and picked up the candies and they began to flower your hands with sugared stains before you could pick them all up.

(You don't even have a framed picture of them.)

Across

7 Kind of cry
It could be sob, pout, or like a cry of joy, or ecstasy, or a silent cry, like the ones that never get past the throat, and never really go away either, what is the word for that?

The old woman stops and swallows.
(She lay awake, nothing had happened for a while. None of the other girls seemed to be awake. The cabin was dark and the upper bunk felt like a shelf in a hot warm cave. No one cared if she was awake or not. It was night, the dark warm night.

She did let her hand slide to her lower belly, where it was damp. This was a cave within a cave. Her pajama pants stretched across her young pelvis.

She did let her fingers massage the little coarse hairs there.

Someone turned in her sleep and she stopped. Nothing happened again.

Her fingertips moved farther down, and she sunk her pelvis into the thin mattress, feeling a hollow there, at the base of her spine, a kind of hungry hollow. She traced circles on the edges of her thighs, and then she closed her eyes tight and she did let her hand touch her, the wet sticky gross red wrinkled real her.

She opened her eyes, still nothing had happened and still everyone slept. She vaguely wished it would be night forever.)

Across

20 A support group, for short

I hate these ones, these acronyms these big letters that stand for long words that stand for the names of things that stand for big spider webs of more stand-fors.

Like AL ANON AL anon. Too many letters.
The old woman puts her hand to her head.
No, I won't tell. No, I won't tell. ANON. They are not even my stories to tell.
(But then she finds herself leaning into him (oh, him), resting her head where it fits just right between his shoulder and his breast. "This one woman said tonight she used to dump out her dad's bottles of Everclear and fill them with water when she was a little bitty girl, she thought he would never know." His chest chuckles a little. She can't stop now. She feels bad, but she cannot stop. "A man said his mom was passed out dead drunk on the front porch the first time he brought home his new wife." His chest doesn't chuckle but he says: "Can you imagine?" and she snuggles closer, her head between his shoulder and sternum, she smells soap and salt and does not imagine.

Later in the meeting, the same man said how his daughter used to get up at 2 a.m. to get ready to leave for school at 6 a.m., so that she would look perfect, and that's when he knew something was wrong.

But she does not say this to him. She rolls onto her back. It's 12:36 a.m.)
They are not even my stories to tell.

Down

20 "The heavenly coffee," first word only.

The song was on TV. Chock full o'Nuts is the heavenly coffee, heavenly coffee. . . . Was it? She never watched TV, she always read. Does Chock fit?

The old woman remembers the song, the taste. They only had canned coffee on vacations, when they were camping, or staying in cabins, or at motels with scratched mirrors when they went to the East Coast family weddings. And funerals.

(She needs two cups to be ready. She needs two cups to lose those images. The dream, again, of the four horsemen as baroque statues she is trying to climb. She can smell the stale coffee in her mouth as the acolyte walks down the aisle. Is this the beginning of death? He has milky skin.)

The old woman puts the pencil down again; the sun is falling fast into the kitchen. The pencil rolls off the table in that sided, punctuated way pencils roll and lands on the floor. The old woman sighs at the distance of the linoleum beneath. The pencil is under the table. It is far away and down and blurring away. She pulls her glasses off and sets them on the paper, below the crossword.

(Did it really happen? In that crowded, hot old house after some distant cousin's winter wedding? Did that man press into her in an upstairs hallway, grab her new breasts and laugh like a child?)

"No, I won't tell," she shakes her head and her voice sounds fermented; the syllables are ripe and oozing.

I am just a batty old lady. Memories are not even. I won't tell, but I guess might as well now. No dead dogs here. No hot water to burn.

The old woman puts her fingers to her sinking mouth. Just please let this be Idaho. Let there be six more days of this dark, and I will be good forever.

The old woman still stares at the crossword. It is fuzzy without her glasses, but not as fuzzy as the pencil on the floor. She thinks she reads

18 Down, "The Arc of the—."

But she can't be sure.
She can't be sure she stood in this kitchen, years or maybe months ago. Her granddaughter, grown and visiting. Her son's daughter. Her son, sober too late. Grandma, she says. Tells her something so unspeakable, *It happened*, that she covers her own mouth and then her granddaughter's mouth, as if to shove the words back in. Back down from wherever they came. Those dark nights. As if she could unmake the girl's memory of her own father's touch. Unmake her body.

Too hot that day as they both stood crying. Never see it, if it hurts too much.

How she had wanted a drink then. But she waited for the girl to leave. They were all supposed to be recovered. But she still kept a bottle in the back of the freezer.

It was easier that way.

19 Across, Shade of yellow

These stories are not even mine to tell, they were maybe, but now they are just voices without bodies, or they had bodies once but only for one day in one room. Now they are just the thin shell-piece secrets of people's cracked-egg hearts. Brown eggs and white eggs and bright pink Easter eggs, they all have the same sunny pupils.

(These stories are secrets, and when they had bodies, they were hot secrets—they were at least 98.6 degrees. Now they are cold, no bodies, no faces even. Just little, little words kept in a jar under the window that the cat paws at. They are just hiding a while till . . .)

The old woman puts her glasses back on. The kitchen is still empty. She does not want to but she reads Across 23, A popular stacking game. It starts with a J. She is probably too old to know it. She sighs. I am too old. She sighs. The milky skin, the jar new. (The things said. Right in this kitchen.)

28 Down, A type of joke

One day, the three and a half minutes of loneliness will become this empty house and the cat will finally knock the jar, whose shininess in the morning sun has perturbed his feline sleep for cat years. He will paw it onto the floor, and the secrets will spill out and they will scatter, a few will break.

But most will heat up a little from the crash.

30 Across, Like some hair

They will not look for their bodies; they are gone maybe.

32 Down, The early years

They are getting hotter. If they are too thin, will they burn?

33 Across, Nihil Longe

They have been waiting for this cat; this black and gray grid, this slanted, sun-filled moment.

52 Down, Old Woman, to Stravinsky

(The cat brushes his claws at the jar,
The woman kicks her toe at the pencil,
The sun warms the black and gray paper until it smells like a hot warm cave.)
Never enough spaces for the word she wants to put.

56 Across

Like a tombstone.

Frog Prince

My best friend saw his own ghost and then I saw him. Two months after he died. He stood across the room, still and silent in the corner, a specter of smoky lace. I walked slowly to him but he vanished well before I could reach out my hand to feel his absence, before I could blow that vision gently into the dust floating in the sunlight coming through the window.

Next, I saw him walking down the street. As I drove by, a face turned to follow my car and when I looked in the rearview it was his dark moony eyes I saw. He would have loved this, his haunting of me. Himself haunted.

Finally he came at night, like a good ghost, floating above my bed, just above the surface of my body like my skin was black water and he was the mist coming off of it. I feared drowning and sat up choking on air, my gasp sending his cloud scattering. After I caught my breath I said his name into the darkness. Ewan.

My voice hoarse and foreign like I, too, was without a body.

*   *   *

Six months before this night where my body was water, he had come to me. Early in the morning, he had tapped at my window.

I had pushed open the thin metal frame and held the cut screen up for him as he shimmied in and landed like a fish on the floor. I expected him to belly up grinning, as he usually did, but he just rolled right over into child's pose and I pulled the pink wool blanket from my bed and lay next to him.

Boo, I whispered.

I slept with someone, he said, turning to look at the ceiling with its fading glow-in-the-dark stars. A man.

I let out a *whoop* and then had to cover my own mouth so my mother wouldn't hear. I giggled and got up on my elbows so I could see his face, his freedom, but he crumbled under my grin. He sobbed for two hours. He kept saying: I'm so ashamed, Elle, I'm so ashamed. I rocked him and rubbed his back and told him, No, no, no. It's good, I said. It's natural. I said. If it was shameful, it wouldn't feel so good. No. God made it feel good. I said. He said, No, Elle, no, I don't want to be like this. I am disgusting, he said.

You are perfect, I said. I love you, I said. Sssshhh, I said. Sweet Prince, I said. I said it over and over until I sweated through my night shirt and he quieted down to sleep.

*   *   *

I met Ewan in second grade. Boy milky and sad. Large eyes the color of coal. I used to let him try my dresses on upstairs in my bedroom in secret and when he had them over his head I would swarm around him and tie the bows, smooth the skirts, and pull him in front of the mirror. I would whisper to him: You are beautiful. He would smile shyly and turn to me. I would bend and kiss him lightly on the cheek. *Poof*, he'd say, and turn back to the mirror grinning. Princess, I'd whisper.

*   *   *

His funeral was small, out on a bluff over the sea on a sunny cold day. His mother and father throwing the ashes into the wind, and me wanting to dissipate too into the air, particle by particle. My mother holding my shoulders so tightly I thought they would crack and I wanted them to. I wanted someone to finally break me in half. For there to be a snap and her left with the pieces of me saying, Oh.

In my anger, this is what I thought they had done to him, but they hadn't seen it was so simple. A snap and then an Oh. Oh.

Oh.

*   *   *

Ewan was seventeen and the man he slept with six months before his death was near forty. He'd found Ewan at the family restaurant he worked at. He was at dinner with his wife but he kept eyeing Ewan, Ewan enjoying it, feeling wanted. Before the man left, he caught Ewan by the arm as he came out of the kitchen and pinned him against the wall. He licked his earlobe as he put his business card in the front of Ewan's belt. Ewan didn't tell me any of this until the morning after he'd finally called the man, ten days after the restaurant. But when he woke up on my floor that morning, his face red and puffy, he told me every detail in one unbroken stream his eyes looking not at me, but at the edge of the blanket I'd pulled over us.

I am a piece of shit, he said.

*   *   *

My mother caught us once, Ewan in pink tulle and me shuffling through a pile on my closet floor for a pair of dress shoes for him. We had the same size feet. When I stood up and turned around, I saw my mother in the doorway locking eyes with Ewan's mirror image. His face ripening crimson. He finally looked at me then hung his head, trying to pull the dress off. I glared at my mother and turned him around to unzip him. She opened her mouth, then shut it. I continued to stare at her with a fierceness she probably didn't recognize, until she left the room.

Poof.

*   *   *

Before he had been cremated, I'd seen him once at the funeral home. His mother holding my hand and guiding it to his cold dead heart. Her hand was warm and bony and I wanted right away to be alone with him. Lie on top of his body and let all of my memories seep into him. To make my body as empty of secrets as his was now. To forget it all together.

*   *   *

When we were in sixth grade, three boys grabbed me after school. I was walking home, crossing the large back field and up the hill to duck through a gap in the fence and onto my street. It was only a five-minute walk but I'd stayed after school to wait out front with Ewan for his mom to come, and she was late. When she'd finally pulled up, we were the last ones waiting and the parking-lot monitor in her orange vest had scolded Ewan's mother's car, glaring at the bumper like it was to blame. After he got in, and I told his mom I'd walk home, the monitor said to me, You, you git on home now, as if she knew of the danger ahead. But I stood still until he turned to wave goodbye to me through the glass, his face smiling through its sadness. A small face with huge lashes and a sweep of black hair that I can still see today, disappearing in the clouds reflected in the window as the car turned out onto the road.

A voice behind saying to me, Now git, sugar, now git.

*   *   *

When he overdosed, his mother called me at dawn to tell me. I was awake, and when the phone rang I knew that it would be her and I knew what she would say. Isn't that what people say? But I did know; I didn't want to get it. It felt like my body was wood as I walked to the ring and my limbs became icy by the time I finally picked it up. It felt like glaciers could form in my bones, had formed, in the time it took me to say hello. I was surely rock when she told me he was gone.

*   *   *

The boys were in the back corner of the field, a brown and sunken soccer ball slapped between them. They were a year older and I had seen them all before. My mom managed a garden store, and I knew one of them was the son of a woman who worked for her. I'd seen him waiting for her to get off her shift. A few years ago, even, we'd played hide-and-seek among the potted citrus trees. His name was Greg, I knew.

*   *   *

Ewan had lost five pounds with that card weighing heavy in his pocket. He couldn't stop thinking about the way the man smelled as he pressed his body up against him, licked his ear. Finally, he drank himself into bravery one night and called the number. The man pulled up outside the restaurant an hour later; Ewan had sobered himself a bit. The man took him to a penthouse apartment right on the shore. The man was a realtor, Ewan said, and as he showed Ewan the opulent rooms he didn't smile. He didn't flirt as he talked about square footage, morning sun, thick walls for privacy. Ewan began wondering if there had been a mistake when they reached the master bedroom and the man undid his pants, pushing my beautiful Ewan to his knees on rough burgundy carpet.

*   *   *

His mom told me everything, how they'd found his body in a park, how the police had come to her house and sat in her living room, My damn living room, she said, Where you kids used to, and her voice raised into a wail. I listened to her cry over the phone and for five minutes, I said *sssshhh* into the receiver. *Sssshhh*. I was rock, I was ice, I was wood, I was a tree but the sound of my leaves in the wind was soothing to the broken mother. I was *sssshhhing* when my own mother, knowing the same way I did, came up the stairs, sat on my bed next to me, and pulled the phone away from my ear. I splintered at the waist and fell sideways into her lap and she held the phone to her ear and said *sssshhh* into the receiver and to me though I was silent and she ran her hand over my hair in firm strokes though I could still feel her own trembling underneath, could still hear the disembodied sobbing on the other end.

*   *   *

I knew as I climbed the hill, as I approached the fence, that the boys were watching me. It's an old story, the way men watch women. Even little men. I kept my pace steady, some prey instinct telling me that if I broke into a run it would bring them on me faster.

And just maybe, I thought, maybe. I remember counting, knowing that I'd be at the fence, through the bushes, onto my street before I got to ten. One. I could see their shifting, hear one snort a laugh. Two. Could smell the way autumn had suddenly arrived. Three. A certain turn in the air. Four. It was getting dark early. Five.

*   *   *

Ewan said, It wasn't like he raped me. Maybe that first blow job, he said, was a little forceful but everything else was welcomed, wanted, wished for. He told me under the blanket: It was so good. I waited for him to find a smile, a giggle, but his face stayed set in its self-punishment. He scowled when he talked about waking the man before he left, doing it all one more time. He met my eyes, But never again. I'm going to be straight for good now, he said. No, I said. He said, God, Elle, God, and sat up. I said, But you are you. Elle, he said, think of my mother. He knelt before me. No, I said. He said, Elle, it would kill my father. He stood over me. *Kill* him.

*   *   *

Once I saw his ghost outside my window. I heard him tapping at the glass in my sleep and I opened the window and pushed through the hole in the screen and landed on the wet grass. He was young again, maybe twelve, always small for his age, and he stood in my yard smiling that sad smile. His big dark lashes. Black, black hair. Ewan, I said. He tilted his head. Ewan, I said again, going to my knees so I'd be his height. I opened my arms and he recoiled. Stepped back a little and I knew it was because of my size. I was large, grotesque, grown the way we never thought we would be at that age. My breasts bare beneath my white night shirt. He shook his head. I covered my chest, my nipples poking through the worn cotton. Ewan, I said, one more time before he turned to run away. Vanishing just before he reached the line of darkness at edge of the yard.

Poof.

*   *   *

They got me at eight. At six, I turned and saw them coming and I started to run. At seven, one grabbed my backpack, and at eight I was on the ground. Nine. One pulled my dress up and my stretch pants down, tearing them over my hips. Ten. Why was I still counting? Eleven. The sky, look at the sky. Twelve. Go away in your head. Thirteen. It's not you they are doing this to. Fourteen. Don't listen to them chanting, Little Pussy, little pussy. Fifteen. Turn your head to your backpack lying next to you. Sixteen. Don't you remember how you are already picking it up, limping home, and, Seventeen, this is already over?

*   *   *

After that morning, Ewan and I didn't see each other for a while. He said he was working a lot, but I knew it was because he had told me what had happened. I was now a party to his shame, it lived outside his memory. I knew this because when he hadn't returned my calls for a couple of weeks I went to the restaurant and sat in a green pleather booth. When he came out of the kitchen and saw me, his face looked panicked. He grabbed an ice water and came over, setting it down in front of me and asking me dryly, what was I doing there? As if he were asking if I wanted some bread. It was like I was the man, the realtor. I was his secret.

Ewan, I said, Ewan. He sat down on the edge of the bench across from me. His body turned outward toward the aisle. I shouldn't have told you, he said. I shouldn't of, he trailed off. He rubbed the back of his neck, turned, put his elbows on the table and his eyes finally met mine. Eyes tired but glittering cold before he pressed his palms into them, his head bent down and his fingers fanned upward like a crown.

My secret was that he could be as cruel to me as he was to himself and I would still love him.

*　　*　　*

Only the largest of the three boys got on top of me. He was twice my size and didn't know what he was doing, I realized later, or didn't want to know. He didn't even push himself fully inside me, but rather underneath me, between my buttocks. He humped for the spectacle and one of the other boys pinned my arms and grunted with him. He made a loud finishing whelp and got up. It was later at home that I saw I was sticky really only on my butt cheeks. Sore only really on my thighs where his pelvic bones had rested. The other grunting boy made to undo his pants and might have actually penetrated me but the third boy spoke up. Hey guys, he said, someone's coming. Come on, come on, let's go. I looked up from my backpack. Greg, Greg's panicked face, saying, Go, go, I saw someone, go. When I rolled over onto my side, I saw no one. I was alone and half-naked in the field and it was fall. I pulled my leggings all the way off, pulled my underwear up and my dress down, brushed the grass away, and grabbed my backpack up off the ground.

I could taste a grassy acid in my mouth as I ducked under the fence.

*　　*　　*

I left the restaurant that day without ordering anything. Ewan called a few days later to apologize, but he wouldn't make plans, either. Said he was working too much. Said he didn't want to talk about it. Said he'd been busy. I was busy too, working for my mom, and a month went by before I surprised him at the restaurant again. When I finally did, I wished I hadn't. When I walked in, early in his shift, I saw him laughing and flirting with a white blond hostess. It was confusing to watch; he pushed her lightly on the arm, she giggled and took a step toward him before turning away, tossing her ponytail, then looking back at him and smiling. Him looking like she was *killing* him. I watched them over customers' heads: the two stood under a brighter light and suddenly I felt like I was watching someone I knew so well on a stage I'd never noticed before. He didn't see me, he disappeared into the kitchen and when he came back I knew right away he was high. Knew by the way he hadn't seen me come in, hadn't called, the way he moved his hands up and down his arms like he was cold, the way he had flirted. Or at least now I think I knew then.

*   *   *

When I got home that day from school my mother asked me what had happened to my leggings and I told her that they had torn on the monkey bars. She shook her head and snatched them from my hand, holding them up. Cheap stuff, she said. I think I can fix them, she said, if you want. Okay, I said. And I went upstairs to the bathroom to wash myself gently, quietly, with a damp red washcloth. It was then I looked in the mirror and realized I was still counting. Very slowly.

I stopped at 209.

*   *   *

By the time he died, Ewan's mother hadn't seen him in three months. She wanted to know if I had. I had but told her I hadn't. Even though I wanted to tell her when I saw him: He looked terrible, your beautiful boy looked terrible. Your beautiful GAY boy was no longer two years sober and looked terrible and it's all your fault. I wanted to call her a bigot. Though I knew that wasn't true. That if Ewan had had the guts to tell them, they would have still loved him. That it was him that didn't want to be different. Him he couldn't run away from, no matter how much he tried. He walked around like his skin was made of slimy shame.

*   *   *

Ewan was the only one who knew my secret. I told him a week after it happened. He was looking for a puzzle to do and pulled the stretch pants from the old toy box where I'd stuffed them after my mom sewed and washed them. He pulled them out and raised an eyebrow and I tore them from his hand. He called me *catty*, What's the matter you on your period or something? I called him *fag* and told him to get out of my house. The next day I found him at recess by a tree in front of the school and he turned away from me so I sat down and told the whole story to his back. He turned back toward me when I got to the part about how I counted, and held my hand when I said only one of them did anything. How he really did nothing, so it wasn't a big deal. It was just humiliating. Ewan hugged me and said, Yes, they did. Yes, it was a big deal. I started to cry, my face hot with a sudden shame, and he pulled away and kissed my lips so gently that I thought for certain that this would be the moment when everything would change. He could be him, and I could be me but, somehow, we could still be together.

Poof.

*   *   *

A few days later I asked if he could forgive me for calling him the
worst possible thing. Yes, he said, he did. And I forgave him later
for closely watching those three boys. For, I thought, having the
luxury to wish what had happened to me had happened to him.
There was so much we didn't say out loud.

*   *   *

His mother told me if I wanted to I could say a few words at the
funeral. I wanted to tell the people gathered there, friends and
family and people from their church, who Ewan really was. How
sure I was that he was better than them. I wanted to tell them a
story, to say Once Upon a Time, there was a boy so beautiful he
would make you weep. When the time came and my mother held
me and asked me if I was ready, I nodded, shaking. But when I
went to speak, no words came out. My silence, my open empty
mouth made them turn away. One older woman sobbing.

They could not know. Not really.

*   *   *

Two years earlier, my mother sent me to a summer camp for a
month. An all girls' camp. She didn't say it, but I knew she was
hoping it would make me less shy. There was swimming and
tennis and sailing lessons, and the girls in my cabin were silly
and nice. Lighthearted in a way I wasn't. But immature in a
way I was. For the first time in years, I didn't somewhere in the
back of my mind feel those boys still watching me. I felt like I
could breathe.

When I came home from camp, I had six new cross-knot

bracelets tied around my wrist, fraying and faded from sun and water. I had just put my bag on my bed, and was breathing in my room, its familiarity, when my mom stood in my doorway and told me Ewan was in the hospital. Well, she said, it was like a hospital. His parents had found cocaine, a bag of it in his room, my mom said. There were other things, other drugs, too. The place he was at would help him. He would be home in a few weeks before school started, she said, but I could write him a letter. Elle, she said, I hope you never. She stopped and looked at me, her arms wrapped around her stomach.

But she needn't have worried, Ewan hadn't even told me his secret, and certainly didn't share it.

*   *   *

Ewan called me for the last time from his ex-boss's phone and told me he was at the restaurant. He said he wanted to say sorry. I hadn't seen him in over two months. Don't leave, I said. I'm coming. I don't know, he said. Ewan, I said, I just want to hug you.

When I walked in I almost didn't recognize him, he was sitting in a booth in the corner with a glass of ice water and some bread his boss, Rick, had brought out. He was thin with dark circles under his eyes. Nothing like the beautiful boy from my bedroom floor five months before.

Poof.

You look terrible, I said, without surprise. You look you, he said, an old joke falling sadly between us as he played with a straw wrapper, balling up the paper into small wads.

What have you been up to? I asked and immediately wished I hadn't.

Look, Elle, he said, sorry I've been a fuck-up. It's just, you know, it's just . . .

It's just me, Ewan. He nodded and scratched the inside of his elbow, he wore long sleeves but I knew what I'd see there if he pulled them up. After he got out of rehab, he came to my house one night and we sat on my bed and he told me everything. He told me about heroin. He said, It was like I was bigger than I am, and in that extra space inside my body, in that extra space, I was exactly who I wanted to be: happy. So happy. I had nodded self-consciously and picked at the knot of one of my new friendship bracelets. I knew I was naïve, sheltered.

I . . . it's just you wouldn't understand. He threw one of the paper wads into his still full water glass.

I know I wouldn't, I said. Because I'm boring.

What I wanted to do was reach across the table and slap him, to tell him he'd been a bad friend. I wanted to tell him how many times I'd called him when he hadn't called at all. To tell him that my crush from geology class had finally talked to me, how he'd called me a *cutie*. How working for my mom was really draining, how I saw Greg's mom every day and how she talked about him all the time, like we were friends, like she wanted to set us up. I wanted to quit and get a job with a stranger, but I didn't know how to. I wanted to tell him I could help him, if he'd just let me.

You're not boring, Elle, he said. You are sweet.

Before I could spit any of my frustration back at him, he reached to me and touched my hand, playing with my fingers. It's just that, he said, sometimes I see myself as this other me. This me that had kept on with lacrosse and debate like my Dad wanted, this me that dates (and the way he looked at me here I knew he meant me), that dates a girl. And that me, this ghost me, is who everyone loves, he's who I'm meant to be. But ever since that night, and there have been more, Elle, ever since that night that me is gone, and it's just me left and so now I'm the ghost.

His voice rasped and I squeezed his shaking hand and knew right then and there that'd I ride this out with him, that I wouldn't fight him or save him. Wouldn't even try for fear he'd stop telling me things like this. And I knew this made me a bad friend, that this was a weak way to love. I knew this and still I leaned over and lightly kissed his cheek. *Poof.*

I wanted him to grin, but he only smiled his sad smile.

*　　*　　*

The last time I saw his ghost I tried to strangle it. I reached my hands through the pale dawn of my bedroom to his throat and tried to kill him forever. He'd been dead one year when he came in the window that last morning. I watched him cross my bedroom and sit at the edge of my bed, hands folded in his lap. He seemed more flesh than ever. He turned to me with his sad eyes and I said, Stop, Ewan, stop, and he hung his head low at this and suddenly I felt grief bubble up in me from years back. I saw that the sadness I'd seen in him since we were children had been my sadness all along. That he'd been keeping it for me all this time so I would have it in these months. Ewan, I said, and my own ghost seemed to rise up in me and lunge to the end of my bed at him, to claw my hands around his shoulders, and to scream Ewan, take it back. Take it back. I coughed, I cried out, I felt sick with the motion of spirit and body and let the sadness come up and out of me, let it grow over my body like moss.

And then he was gone. My hands empty and wet. I felt like a broken shell as my mother pushed through my door. *SSSHHHH*, she said, picking me back up, pulling me up to the top of my bed. Just a dream. *Sssshhh*. As she got in bed beside me and hugged my sweaty head to her chest, I saw she was still half-asleep, saw that I was her child again. She closed her eyes and hummed lightly in her dream, a lullaby that told me I would carry the empty sound of his name inside me the rest of my life.

Ewan.

*   *   *

That last day he had walked me out to my car. At the front entrance of the restaurant, between two sets of doors, we passed the gumball machines and he grabbed my elbow. Got a quarter? he asked, and I dug into the bottom of my purse until I found two. I gave him one and he put it in the machine next to the gumballs, the one with small plastic bubbles with toys in them and cranked the knob. He got a blue bubble with a pink beaded bracelet inside. I went next and got a temporary tattoo of a heart with a golden bird flying over it. He placed the bracelet over my wrist, gentle as always, pulling it over my watch.

Come home with me, I said. He kept my hand in his as we pushed out into the parking lot. It was windy, and you could smell the ocean. A damp brine.

You need a warm bed, I said. A bath. I wanted to keep him under the blanket on the floor again. I wanted him to let me hold him. Come, come on, come on, I said, and pulled him toward my car. Come on, I was in a hurry now, looking for my keys but not letting go of his hand, Yes, I said, just for a night, Yes, yes, I was talking fast. As if I already knew that we didn't have much time left together. He stopped walking and dropped my hand.

I can't, Elle, he said. I just, he looked across the parking lot toward a maroon sedan idling. I just, I have to go. But I'll call you soon, I promise.

No, I said. I could feel my chin quivering, my voice bare branches. Trembling. No, you won't.

I grabbed his hand again.

Elle, come on, really.

I pressed the tattoo into it. He pulled away and grinned. Love you, he said and took off jogging toward the car. I didn't see who was driving, man or woman.

I stayed in the empty parking lot for a few minutes until I heard that voice deep within me saying, Now git, sugar, now git.

As if we could outrun our own nightmares.

*   *   *

That day at the funeral home, when his mother finally unclasped my hand over his dead heart, I asked her if I could have a moment. Her mouth gaped open as if I had asked to hold the child in her womb but then she slowly nodded. When she left the room, I did not lay on top of him. I did not say the things I wanted to. I straightened his tie. I smoothed the mossy green suit around his limbs. I took the pink beaded bracelet from my wrist and tucked it in his breast pocket. I put my hand over his. I put my other hand on his head, careful not to mess his hair. I closed my eyes and I saw him waving in the car window. Me, waiting.

Two children.

I opened my eyes and saw his gray face and told him, Ewan.

You are beautiful.

I leaned over to kiss him on his cold lips.

And it was just as sad as you imagine it when you fail to save someone.

Poof.

Six and Mittens

*T*oday is the day of the party. The party for me, because I am six. It is a princess cat party. It will be FUN, mom says. Maybe it will be but I don't know. I wanted to just invite Six and Mittens but Mom made me invite REAL friends. She cannot see Six and Mittens. They are real, but she cannot see them so we have to invite REAL friends like cousin Jeanie and Taylor from down the street.

Sometimes a friend is a kid you barely know.

Six says it's okay he's not invited, even though this is really a party for him, since he is a six, and I am only just turning six. Mittens hates this. Mittens thinks I should lock myself in the closet. Mittens is a cat, and she doesn't like REAL people. Sometimes she tells me I should be a cat. And when I pet her soft fur and listen to her purr which helps me sleep it's true that I wish I was her kitten because she wouldn't get after me about having REAL kitten friends. She thinks Mom is a real PROBLEM. Not to be trusted. Mom says, This is a PROBLEM. *This* is Six and Mittens. The problem is that they are REAL to me, but not REAL to Mom. What should be, says Dr. O, is that they are imaginary to me. Then Mom wouldn't care if they came to the party though Dr. O says that because of the way Mom's brain works, which is like everyone else's brain but mine, she will always like REAL friends like Jeanie and Taylor better than Six and Mittens. I don't know why she can't see them. But neither could Dad before he went on VACATION and neither can Dr. O.

The party is going to be in the backyard. There are already balloons tied to the folding chairs Mom got out of the basement. Red, Blue, and Purple. I wanted Purple Purple Purple but Mom said No because Jeanie and Taylor are REAL and they have their own favorite colors. There is Half-Full Honeybear on the folding table, who is my friend also and who I said had to come this morning. I cried and fitted about it. Half-Full Honeybear asked me to come. I could not say no because I eat his honey every day on my wheat toast with margarine. Mom said okay but NO BALLOON FOR HIM. So I rinsed off his sticky bottle with warm water and put him on the table. Mom can see the honeybear, but he is not a REAL friend. This is different than Six and Mittens, because she cannot see them at all. We got a special pink tablecloth with white cartoon cat princesses on it for the party. The sky is blue today. Dr. O will not be at the party though she is REAL and my friend. Maybe she doesn't like balloons.

Mom says she can't believe I am six!

Before the party, I play with my friends. I have drawn Mom a million pictures of Six and Mittens and still she says they are not REAL. I have told her: Six is a feeling, a noise, and a bubbly blue number who curls in my neck. Mittens is a tabby cat, a big one, with green eyes just like the one Aunt Tammy has but bigger and with greener eyes. I have said, Mom, look, Six is cuddling you, and still she can't see him. Six says it doesn't hurt his feelings but it hurts my Mom's. Once I started crying because Mittens was sick, and Mom wouldn't take her to the animal doctor like she takes her pet bunny Flopsy, and she finally yelled, I cannot take her because SHE IS NOT REAL, and I said she was the meanest mom in the world and that she loved Flopsy more than me, and she got quiet and sent herself to her room for a while and she came out with her face all messy. I gave her a hug but she didn't hug back because she was holding her head. The she did hug back, real hard. She said she was going to call Dr. O first thing in the morning.

Mom says I am sick.

That's why I see Dr. O. It's my brain that's sick and it's called childhood SCHIZOPHRENIA which is very rare. Six and Mittens are why I am sick. They don't feel bad about this because they are my friends. Before Dad went on VACATION he got very angry. He told Mom that she was crazy. He told me I was not sick but that really I was a BAD kid.

Sometimes he was a Dad and sometimes he was a Sorry.

Dad and I look alike. Brown hair. Blue eyes. Dad will not be at the party because he is still on VACATION and it's the kind of VACATION that goes on and on and on. Mom sometimes finds something that belongs to my Dad and puts it in a box in the garage. Like a shirt of his in the trunk of the car. It was his Steelers t-shirt. It is in the box now. I check every day to see if it is still on top and I smell it and it smells like my dad, like sour vanilla and also like the trunk of the car. Rubbery.

Mittens says we should burn that box. But Six hates fire. Me too. It's hot and it burns. Mittens doesn't mind it though.

Mom says Mittens is a BAD friend.

Jeanie and Taylor come to the party on time and they sit with their moms who were also invited. We eat the cake and play bobbing for apples. I wanted a piñata but mom said NO DICE and NO BASEBALL

BATS. But I get an apple almost first try and Taylor never gets one and Jeanie takes forever and looks funny with her red hair all crazy from getting a little wet. They each give me presents. Taylor a game called Uno, which is nice because Taylor, who has a million freckles, says after I open it that he and his mom got it because they know I like numbers. Then Jeanie gives me a pink-wrapped present with a purple sparkly bow that I like and I open it and it's a Malibu Barbie who is kind of dumb looking but okay I guess. The best thing is that then Taylor shows us how to rub our balloons on our hair until it sticks up and we are all laughing even though I sort of don't like the way the balloon makes my hands smell. It's not like medicine but it is kind of. It reminds me of the day they put me in the box of light so they could look at my brain and I couldn't move or blink. After I remember that I don't want to play with the balloons anymore so I let mine go, go, go. Off the string undone, gone, up to the blue blue sky and off to birthday land. Taylor says OH NO, but it's not an oh no, and Mom says: It's time for cake! They sing "Happy Birthday" to me and Jeanie says, Samantha make a wish! Taylor shouts, Yeah Sam! And so I wish that my party would be every day not because of the balloons or the cake but because I am laughing and my mom is laughing and she is leaning over and kissing my head and whispering, Happy birthday sweetheart and Yes, make a wish. And she smells like lemon soap and I want to sleep in that smell. We eat cake and then Jeanie says, Let's play with your new Barbie! And her mom who looks like a clown, big hair, nose, lips and everything red, red, red, helps us take Barbie out of the box which is impossible but we finally get her free. I want the Barbie to play Bobbing for Apples but Jeanie, says, Noooo! You'll mess up her hair! So I let her play with the dumb doll in the grass while Taylor and I look at a potato bug he found in the dirt until it's time for them to go home.

Mom says the party was a WILD SUCCESS. It's nice when Mom is so happy. I know she loves me. But I'm exhausting to love. All kids are. But especially me.

She lets me have another piece of cake after everyone leaves and some time to play alone with Six and Mittens, and of course the first thing we do is play bobbing for apples. The metal trough which in other summers had dirt and flowers in it is still filled with water and red apples in the yard and Six is very good at it but Mittens won't play. She wants MORE friends to come and suddenly Dog 123 is there, and Maple Lace, who is a dancing squirrel, is there too.

There are so many friends I know I must be getting tired. Dr. O says whenever I see a lot of friends that means I need to go lie down. But I don't want to lie down! It's finally like a real party! Like a NORMAL kid would have. Maple Lace is always using the word NORMAL.

Maple is a friend but sometimes a friend is a noise in your brain that hurts. It is her voice that is high that hurts. Today she is telling me the cake was poison. That mom is sick of me. That Dad is coming back from VACATION and will spank me again because I am a BAD kid.

Six tells her to back off and I shout at her NO!

Mom puts her head out the screen door and says, Everything okay? I tell her yes, and she watches me for a minute before she closes the screen.

In a minute, I hear the phone ring, and Mittens starts telling me that Flopsy wants to go swimming. Maple says, Yep, that's true. Six barely mumbles anything and I tell them, It *is* sad that no one ever lets Flopsy go swimming, not even in the bathtub!

Even I get to go swimming.

We get Flopsy out of her wire cage in the corner of the yard that has hay in the bottom and a wood box for her to sleep in. Flopsy always scratches my arms when I pick her up because she can't help it. She is so soft. Like Mittens. Her ears are long and feel like velvet. I put her in the water trough and wonder if she will try to swim after the apples that are still in there.

Just so you know, rabbits can swim just fine.

A minute or so later, we are all singing the "Happy Birthday" song to me and watching Flopsy swimming away when Mom comes out onto the back stoop with the cordless to tell me my Dad is on the phone and wants to wish me a happy birthday but then she sees Flopsy in the water and screams. She's holding the phone in her hand but drops it and runs to Flopsy, pretty much knocking us all over to get to her. She's fine, I try to say, but Mom yanks the bunny from the trough and presses her to her heart, looks at me, and screams YOU!

Now Mom sits on the couch holding Flopsy in an old yellow towel. Her brown and white fur is nearly dry and her nose is twitching for more carrots. Mom has already fed her two. Dad has come back from VACATION. They have me sitting on the floor by the sofa while they talk. I am playing with the cream carpet strings and pulling at them even though I know I'm not supposed to.

Mom is saying she is at her WIT'S END. That Flopsy could have drowned. There's no way out of that bucket for her, she says.

I try to tell her that Flopsy had only been in there a minute.

But she keeps talking. Saying that I am too sick. Dad is nodding, pacing, he turns to me. He hasn't shaved and is not wearing his Steelers t-shirt. Mom says, Maybe we should try another doctor.

Mom never wants me on too many meds, she doesn't want me to be too sleepy. She wants me to be myself. Even though myself is hard. Dad thinks he can fix me himself, which Mom says is a PROBLEM. And it's called DENIAL.

He comes over and shakes me hard. Why? He asks? Why? We

do everything for you! Why? He is not wearing his Steelers t-shirt because it is in the garage. I am glad I cut a piece out of it now.

I tell him that Mittens wanted to see Flopsy swim. And she did! She swam!

He pushes away from me and asks, Mittens? And I nod. Then he yells, THAT'S IT! He throws up his arms.

Mom says, Leave it, she can't help it.

That's it, he says again and now folds his arms, like he might laugh. He looks at my mom and disappears down the hall. We hear him open the door to the basement and his boots on the creaky wood stairs. Eight steps. The laundry is down there. I don't go down there.

Mom glances at me and caresses Flopsy's long gray ears. Six is sleeping he is so bored with this and Mittens is licking her paws on the floor next to me. We hear Dad making noise, moving furniture or something. It's okay, my Mom says, but I don't know who she is talking to.

When he comes back upstairs he has a gun like I have seen on television. He is holding it in his hand, low, down by his waist. My mother sees it and screams, sheltering Flopsy with her hands, moving next to me.

CALM DOWN, Dad says to her, and turns to me. Mom moves closer to me until she is almost on top of me. YOU ARE CRAZY she is screaming. I stay put.

He points the gun at the space next to me.

PUT IT DOWN, Mom is still screaming, like someone on TV.

I stare at him.

Where is Mittens? He asks, his voice is soft and almost nice. Sweetheart?

Right here, I say and point to the floor by my left leg where Mittens has paused in her licking and is looking up at Dad.

There? Dad asks.

I nod.

Are you SURE? Dad asks.

Yeah, I say. Why?

The shot is so loud it almost knocks me over. Mom is screaming. My ears are singing. There is a bullet mark in the carpet and one on the wall. The room smells funny. Mom is saying CRAZY, FUCKING CRAZY and the phone starts ringing. GET OUT, my Mom is screaming and I am holding my hands to my ears and screaming now.

The next thing I know Mom is holding me on the couch and rocking me and it is daylight. I am so tired. Dr. O will be there later, Mom says. I am so tired. Medicine, they must have given me sleepy medicine. Mom tells me I haven't spoken in two days. Dad is there in different clothes and asks me if I want to bury Mittens and Mom gives him a bad look but he keeps talking. Look, he says, we haven't touched him, we left him, and he points to the bullet hole in the carpet, like a black eye.

I snuggle back into Mom and go back to sleep.

When I wake up it's morning and Dad is there again and has dug a big hole in the backyard. Mom takes me upstairs and softly changes my clothes. I let her do everything because I am tired and she leans in and smells so lemony and soapy I almost fall asleep again. She kisses my head after she pulls on my favorite shirt with a sparkly unicorn. Oh Sam, she says. Then she takes me outside, where it's still cold and dewy, leading me by the shoulders to the hole in the corner of the yard opposite of where Flopsy's cage is. The hole is empty and the size of the microwave and Dad is staring proudly in it like it's not just dirt in there. Dr. O is there in a blazer, her hair up on top of her head, and she reaches for my hand. I'm not sure this is a good idea, she starts to say, but Dad glares at her and she curls back like a six. He turns to me and asks if I want to say anything. I have not wanted anything since I woke up and now I want to get in the hole and go back to sleep. I rub my eyes.

Dad starts putting dirt back in the hole when I hear a little laugh. It's Six, and he's rubbing up against my leg.

I take a deep breath.

Dad puts another shovelful in and Mittens hops onto my shoulder. *Ssshhh*, she says.

My chest folds with her weight on my body.

Mom watches me with a sad smile. It's better, she says. Don't you think it's better? And I don't know why but I start crying, and all this stuff is coming out. Breaths and heaves and shudders and cries and I cannot stop it. Mom hugs me and is crying a little too and Dr. O is watching so close. Dad pauses for a minute and is leaning on his shovel and looking proud of himself.

Mom says, My poor sweet girl.

When I stop crying enough to catch my breath, Dad nods at me and starts filling in the hole again. The morning sun is starting to make its way to us. He tosses the dry crumby dirt into the hole, and after another couple of shovel scoops, I notice Maple Lace is here now, dancing behind Mom. One more shovel throw and Dog 123 trots up behind Dad. Another, and a few black cats appear on the fence top behind us. I have calmed down and Mom is rubbing my back and talking about going to the zoo later, my favorite, and Dr. O is saying something about rest and I'm not listening at all because now all of the cats are here, and Maple Lace is laughing, and Dad is patting the dirt with the back of the shovel and saying, It's done, then—but now there are even some new friends in the yard. A rabbit named 1000, and a red number Three. And a number Nine! He's blue! The morning sun is finally out from behind the house and warming us up as two yellow birds appear now above Dr. O's head! I laugh as they tweet around her hair like she's a cartoon who got a big bump on the head.

Mom says, You are feeling BETTER! She leans down and kisses the top of my head.

And I nestle Mitten's soft tabby fur against my right ear and I look around at all my new friends and I nod at her because sometimes a Mom is everything that is right.

And I say: BETTER.

American Grief in Four Stages

One

We knew my sister was really different, after all, the day she got murdered. They found her body in a paper–recycling bin behind some grimy nightclub that had a reputation for playing Serbian folk music set to techno. Turbo-folk, they called it. Someone had cleft off her left breast and pulled out her left front tooth, which had been chipped anyhow when she fell off her bike when we were kids. My parents, of course, were devastated, staring continually at reruns of *The Love Boat*, with my mother occasionally turning to us and saying, "She was se-ven-teen!" before turning back to the TV. We no longer went places, not even to Sunday buffet dinners at the local all-you-can even though we'd always done that. So I told them, after she'd been gone a month or so, I turned down the TV and I said, Look, she's always been different and now, she's dead, while we live. Who knows? I said, Maybe this is just her way of being different again.

Saying this may or may not have helped, all I know is that the next Sunday my mother went to the church down the road, the one with a naked wooden cross, next to the parking lot where my sister had gone over her handlebars and that maybe still contained, somewhere in its gritty black gravel, a tiny chip of her tooth. All these years later, ground to almost nothing. Zip. Zilch. Nada.

Two

I kept thinking maybe it's not a big deal. That she's gone, really. She wasn't really like us, always trying to change us, cooking us protein diet meals so that my parents might trim down, suggesting we go to a video installation at the new art museum, refusing to go the water park on the grounds that she was suddenly too old for that crap, as if we hadn't been doing that every summer of our lives, and as if she hadn't loved it for the last ten years of banana slides and wave pools. As if she really suddenly couldn't stand the cherry-red taste of Tiger's Blood: her favorite snow cone spurned just like the rest of us, just like M's creamy casseroles and P's sawing of two-by-fours, the continual dividing of lengths, the short-short pieces and the very long ones piled all together, the parts for something that would never be built, had not even been imagined, was only an accidental sculpture in the backyard, growing and growing, a new heap of wood now in the front. Jesus, she screamed one night, Either build something or stop, stop, stop. As if she didn't love the sound of it, as if we didn't grow up hearing that rhythmic grating and know that our father was home from work. The grinding and splitting and knocking of the wood, the best bad habit ever. The thing that kept him from the dormant evils of some other past. As if it wasn't kind of funny when he threatened to saw off our arms that one time when he caught us playing naked together in the closet, and we learned. As if he ever really did it, instead of just hanging our bodies, arms hooked over the sawhorse, us kneeling, the sun squinting to see us, the hacksaw impressing us each only a little on our touching arms, him complaining that it wasn't the same. That it was the sound he loved: the Sound of Wood, he screamed as he threw the saw down, not you, not your sound. And we ran up the street to the dead end and down into the dry canal ditch and licked our cuts, and as if that was really all that bad, as if it wasn't a great, character-building moment for all times. A story to tell our own kids someday so they'd know that we, too, had been children. That we, too, had had fathers.

If she hadn't stopped being her, this whole dismembering murder would be sad, devastating, a terrible loss, but wasn't she already just a shell of herself? I mean, why was she at that nightclub anyway? The place had a neon sign that said "ANCE"; the pink *D* burned out. It was gross and when I walked by a month after she was gone, it smelled like stale French fries and wet swimsuits. I mean if she hadn't decided she hated us and that this place with giant, foreign bouncers who hadn't seen a thing was better than watching TV with us, that really anything was better than watching TV with us, then it might be different now.

It's not our fault, you see? It's hers.

Three
It took us a long time to forget my sister. First of all there was her stuff.

A.   Her Stuff: Clothes, cutoffs, old t-shirts, lace pajamas, silk and cotton undies, running shorts, tattered swimsuits, balls of running socks, ribbed tank tops, jean skirts, fuzzy sweaters, flannel boxer shorts, her old pep-club uniform—all of this could go in big black trash bags. The dresses stayed hung in the closet, my mother unwilling to crumple them. She closed the door; I opened it. I suggested we get rid of some of the ones my mother had always thought too slutty and still she shook her head and remembered to me the middle-school stomps and winter balls of years past, and the junior prom whose blue satin was still so practically new that I might wear it someday. I told her that was creepy but she closed the door again on the empty dresses and I closed my mouth but knew I would have to come by night for them.

The bags piled up by the door, ready to go to Goodwill. My mother, standing in front of the shiny heap, became afraid that someone we knew would buy them there, and that she would see my sister's clothes on other bodies with other names or even worse, on strangers. So my father and I drove them to the dump in the old white truck. My father put in his Willie Nelson cassette like he always did for going to the dump, but unlike most trips when the truck came back just as full with my father's found treasures— pieces of corrugated metal in decent shape or rotting file cabinets— the scratched bed stayed empty. He stared at it once we unloaded, then he slammed the bed door shut. The sound rattled and the seagulls cried. There was no talk on the way home, no, Can you believe someone would throw this stuff away? I mean, a perfectly good stove, just sitting there. There was not even any Willie Nelson, no "On the Road Again," or us singing along with exaggerated twangs, just radio static with now and then a faint voice coming in, stuttered enthusiasm for traffic, weather, hourly contests.

B. Then there were her remains. Of course, we'd properly cremated and buried the majority of these but still there were stray parts of her, bodily detritus that kept turning up all over the house. Her hair, red and long, coiled in the drain or stuck to a couch cushion, a whole clot of it swarming my mother's hairbrush. Her fingernails, clipped sloppily and hastily just before she died, left in a pile of tiny moon phases on the bathroom counter. There were, we knew, all sorts of shed skin cells, dandruff dust of hers that we couldn't even see, and so couldn't fully rid ourselves of. A breast, a tooth at large (a murderer too, I knew). Her baby teeth in a little silk box, her ponytail braided and chopped from her first haircut. I even found her pubic hair, red coarse kinks on the under edge of the toilet seat.

Her smell, too, lingered, a combination of cigarettes, strawberry Bubblicious and Chanel No. 5. And some other smell she'd always had, an earthy warm curry of a waft.

There was also the sound of her absence, her nonfootsteps, her nonlaugh, her nonvoice.

Which brings us to C. the Persistent Belief in Her Continued Existence: the mail still came for her, her subscription to Cosmo arrived faithfully. A bill from the clinic for birth control no one knew she was on. A notice that it was time for her to renew her car registration. An advertisement for a sale at a department store. Once in a while a call from the detective saying he wanted to go over a few more details, saying he didn't have any new leads, saying he couldn't figure it.

My mother still bought Carnation Breakfast on the same biweekly basis and the chocolate malt boxes piled up. No one else drank that chalky crap. I even tried, in an effort to reduce the accumulation, and could not do it without hearing my sister clanking the bottom of the glass with a spoon to loose the stuck powder.

We still expected her to arrive, to return, we still thought of ideas for Christmas gifts like an automatic fingernail dryer; and I still became annoyed with her when I awoke suddenly in the night, sure that it was her late and drunken entrance that had disturbed me. For a full year we, when absentminded, would set the table for four.

It took great concentration to remember the absoluteness of her vanishing and yet that was still not the most difficult part of her death.

D. The most arduous step in the effort to forget her was undeniably the myriad of memories, both individual and collective, that inevitably included her. Of course there were the photographs in which her ember hair and lunar face and giant gross toothy smile kept popping up. The dreaded Glamour Touch portrait of her from the mall, smiling with her lips closed for once, head tilted, air-brushed in a gold-colored frame by which my mother kept one single, plastic red rose. Yet we could lay those photos facedown, burn them if at any point they became too much, but nothing could be done about that time when she was a kid and I was a baby and we were at the store and she toddled off and my mother found her topless, eating a bag of Cheetos, the electric orange powder all over her face and fingers and tiny pale torso so that she looked toxic. Nothing could be done about the time she gave me a 900 number to dial and told me it was a direct line to Santa but it turned out to be a phone sex line. She dialed for me and then went into my parents' bedroom to get on the line and listen, and nothing could be done about her stifled giggles as it rang, the way she guided me to go ahead and press one, accept the charges. But then when Santa revealed that he did in fact have a big package for me and I squealed with delight, she yelled, She's a kid you creep, and told me to hang up. Nothing could be done about the time she made my father promise to buy her as-seen-on-TV Sea-Monkeys at the drugstore and when he forgot she refused to come out from under the bed until he told her the truth about Sea-Monkeys, that they were really brine shrimp, and for heaven sakes she deserved a real pet, like a goldfish.

Even memories we considered our very own, the ones we starred in like my thirteenth birthday party at the water park, were suddenly invaded by her, the way she had been there, the way she took all day to get up the courage to go off the Acapulco Cliff Dive and then when she finally did her swimsuit top fell off, giving my friend Chad a boner, and she laughed and cried and said that it was the best thing she had ever done and made up a song about the Acapulco Cliff Dive to the tune of "I Heard It through the Grapevine" that she sang for a week straight. Nothing could be done about remembering the way she'd croak those stupid off-rhythm lyrics while we were doing the dishes or her total victory when she caught me humming the tune one night while brushing my teeth (Ha! she cried, It's a hit, I wrote a hit!), and nothing could be done about wondering if she'd still be alive if she'd been willing to go with us to the drive-in to see *Hannah Montana: The Movie* for my fifteenth birthday.

You see they were constant, these intrusions of her memory, but I knew if we could forget her, if we really could forget her, then not only would she not be alive, she would not be dead. And if she wasn't dead, then we would be happy again. But it was not easy. In fact we had to launch an intensive Future-Talk campaign, initiated by me, where at the dinner table we would only talk about tomorrow, and what we were going to do: Trips we might take, the three of us (all places my sister would have disdained, like Disneyland and Six Flags); Online junk-selling businesses my parents could start one day, or even right after the meal; Places nearby I might go to college; Quilts my mother might stitch; Men I might date whom my father might like; Triumphant family moments to come. We concentrated hard on the food at hand and threw ourselves wholeheartedly into a timespace that had not yet arrived, but that was full of griefless light.

These were the trials of those months yawning into the rest of my high-school career, and yet eventually we did succeed, we did, in forgetting her. My father turned her old room into an office, I quit finding hair, and I remembered solely the spacious only-childness that was now so familiar it might always have been but for a nagging thought, like something I forgot to do, a faint name, an outline of some other head shape in the car window, a face that mine looked more and more like every day.

But this did not happen before the event.

Four

The Event. Mouth drying, throat swelling, the most difficult type of thing to speak of. It was like this. One day I saw her. She was coming out of an IHOP diner in a pink summer dress that looked god awful with her red hair. (My first reaction, in fact, was to balk: my mother always told her to avoid pink, and now she appeared for the first time in months in it.) She was real thin and had a tube in her nose and she looked alone but was walking just behind some family with two small blond kids. Towheads. She was taller than all of them but slouching, carrying a purse that was meant to look like a stuffed animal, a tabby cat, and on the side slung in a strap was a hammer with flowers, daisies, painted on the wooden handle. The sun was glass hot and the light was coming down and then back up in blinding strokes; I squinted hard against it as she turned the other way so that from across the parking lot, shielding my eyes, I broke our family rule and said her name aloud. It almost deafened me. But she didn't even hear it, so I said it again this time louder but it came out softer, possibly because of the ringing in my ears from the first utterance. So I yelled it and found myself hoarse, my throat dry and tight, my voice suddenly empty. I bent over, hands on knees, and smelled my sweat, the syrup from the IHOP, the bacon, and a sick sweet fat became the space between her and me and when I looked up she was gone.

I stumbled to the old Volkswagen red bug, once-hers-now-mine, and I got in and shut the windows and even though it was the kind of day when you couldn't leave a dog or a baby in the car for more than two minutes, I stayed in there for a long time and no one broke the window to save me.

And in there I slipped. I did know, really know, for the first time—with wet-faced convulsions in reference to all those years together, my god all that accumulated proximity of her-near-me and all that siblinial, road-tripian language of which I was the last remaining speaker—I did know that by seeing her just then at an IHOP in whited-out sunlight, dressed in unflattering tones and deaf to me, that I would never see her again. And not only that, I knew too that there would always be some remainder. Her death was divisible by nothing, and I was a leftover and I was left behind, and I was alone at a diner, and elsewhere too in places where my sister might have come with me if she were not dead, but instead she was not alive, and this was a finality that made me ache clearly and loudly and freakishly in, of all places, my left breast.

Origins

She was in the gas-station bathroom, her mother and brother waiting outside by the car—not waiting the way she imagined, still and huddled like horses in the cold, breaths bursting from their nostrils or now, now wolves, feet pawing the ground—while she looked down at the paper-clogged toilet and the stones that had fallen out of her. Ruddy. Brown. Smoothed dull by her thirteen years. She dared not flush. Later her mother would take her to the doctor to learn she would always be small, her pelvis broken, even, by a simple wish for a child and so she would remain. Childless. And her mother would say, Well, start a rock collection. This phrase a substitute for her own broken heart. Burying phantom grandchildren, already. Tiny graves, though. The size of a finger poked in the dirt to make a hole for three sister seeds. Corn. Bean. Now squash. And had she not already done that a hundred seasons?

But her daughter had not.

Each month she threw the stones away, out of her pocket on walks to school, in the trash. She tendered other things. Squirrel on the feeder. Rabbit she fed sugar to from a Dixie cup on the back porch that her brother eventually shot. She buried it and considered the tiny teeth that had nibbled at the thick skin of her thumbprint.

It was not so thick her skin and so she resolved to toughen it. Black leather, jagged hair. Bottles. Boys. Men, even. But this, this neither, could keep her from a truth. Not of the stones but of the place they had come. That bathroom. That place. To discover that there were a million ways to be a mother except for her. Its dinge, promise of vagrance, smell of bleached shit. She felt like that. Childless always and now. A junky. Like the rabbit's bones under the dirt. Rotten. Body stretched thin by needles until. How long will a rabbit live unshot?

There are lots of ways to grow up, to become man or woman, and this was one. Even as her pelvis refused to ripen. Did she try to quit? She must have. Her brother, rabbit-killer, her brother had two pink babies before he was even twenty. They gummed her fingers, left them wet. Pulled the studs in her ears. Stretched her lobes. Reminded her what clean meant, what mother meant. What wasn't hers.

So she didn't quit.

And when she had had enough, she had too much. Heavy hit. And she was back there squatting over the toilet that her mother had told her was too dirty to touch. Her own body too dirty to touch, the stones crumpled into her blood. Sooty blood. Heavy blood.

And now the shapes of meager horses gather, small clouds of cold breath in the night.

And she the wolf. So tired, the wolf.

Extra Patriotic

*H*e had been a soldier and now he was not. It should have been simple but it was not. He lived in the suburbs with his mother, three years out, and his mother liked to say he hadn't quite *settled*. He didn't say anything about it. What it felt like to him, was, at worst: when he was in the Walmart parking lot with his mother, he wanted to tear his skin from his body and walk around, muscle, tissue, half a skeletal face bared because he had seen these things, people without skin, and felt that other people should too. Other Americans. At best: it felt to him like he'd already done this. And then he'd stitched his skin back on a little too tight, crooked stitches running vertical down the middle of the back of his legs, his arms, itching.

The sun was never hot enough.

He had one army buddy, of course he did. They played Minecraft every Wednesday. His buddy was always saying, Get a damn dog, that's what I did. He'd nudge Oatmeal with his good foot, the service retriever the VA therapist had gotten him. It helps, he said, Buddy, it really helps. Not, he said, not for the reason they said it would. They said this stupid fucker would smell my anxiety, would sense my panic episodes kicking in and then do some calming shit, like put his head on my knee. Dumb mother fucker doesn't care if the world is closing in around me. But, it helps, still, because when I walk around, go to the store or whatever, people give me space. They see me and my little fur fucker with his service vest on and they give me space, I don't know if they are afraid of the dog, afraid of distracting the dog, or maybe afraid of me but they see me how I am, different. Wounded. They don't just see me as some regular fucker who maybe sells insurance and didn't see his buddies halved and kilt for no goddamn good reason. And that helps.

And it was true, his buddy loved that dog but it wasn't for him.

Before the war he'd been the kind of guy who laughed real loud, who always drank too much, who didn't listen to other people, like really listen, when they were trying to tell them about themselves. Women, he didn't listen to women. He'd always been sort of good looking and so women were always telling him stuff but he didn't listen. He thought he had, but when he looked back on it now. When he remembered Lacy, his high-school girlfriend, telling him about the time her middle-school tennis coach raped her in the club pool house, opening up her own skin, tears in her eyes like nectar, how she'd never told anyone because the coach had said to her, This is your fault, you little slut. But she told him on the saggy basement couch of her house and he had twirled her hair but didn't really listen.

In other words, he'd been stupid.

Now he owned a gun and he knew what listening was. He knew the sound of his own heartbeat, of course, but of others too. Even Oatmeal, so loud that dog heart, it kept him awake the night he crashed at his buddy's. The sound of the fridge clicking to life, his mother's bed shifting in the night as she tossed and turned, the man down the street opening his garage door, starting his sprinkler system, the tiny beeps right before the water sputtered to life and hushed him to sleep every morning at 5 a.m.

One day he said to himself, Something has got to give, but nothing will. And then another day, not long after that, he met her. Well he saw her. His sister, actually, wanted to introduce her to him. His sister called and woke him up midday. His mouth tasted like blood and she told him she was on lunch break. She worked at a marketing firm. He had chewed his cheek up inside, ground its rubber in his sleep and now it felt like kelp to his tongue. Jesus, she said, you're just waking up? He was used to her disgust, he liked it, it reminded him of what had not changed. Look, she said, you are going to get up, do some fucking push-ups or whatever, shower, shave, and be at my place at six. He grunted, why did his sister always frame things like a movie montage? And why did her life really work out that way, like a movie? A house, a pool, a husband, a labradoodle. Seriously tweek, I have someone for you to meet. He groaned. His mother had said that a million times. But the last one, Mary Jo, talked the whole time over tapas about the scrapbooking business she wanted to start and he wanted to fucking tear his fucking head off until finally at dessert she said, You ARE quiet, and he nodded. And she said, A penny for your thoughts? And he pulled out his phone and she giggled, Are you going to text me? But he pulled up his photos, and found one of an Iraqi that had hanged on the road between base and S— and had his junk removed and his eyes eaten by birds and still no one cut him down. He showed her the one from about a month in, but really, it was a series. His own archive. He kept taking them until he shipped out. By six months, the body was like a strip of beef jerky with hands. Mary Jo covered her mouth and met his eyes and for three seconds he thought maybe she sees me, maybe she will take me in her arms and tell me she is so sorry for my shredded interior but then she threw the phone onto his plate and said under her breath, You Sicko, and left the restaurant.

So he groaned. Shut up, his sister said, this one's great. Maybe more damaged than you, and that's just what you need. He wasn't sure that was it, what he needed, but he knew the way his sister thought. If only he could see that other people were starving, she once told him, while he had a bed and food and soda, then he could be okay, even grateful, and he didn't know how to explain to her that all of what was in his head was completely unrelated to food. She had called him *fucking helpless* and he'd shrugged but then the next week he hadn't eaten at all. Just to see. To see if his mind would clear. Would care. But he'd just slept more. Was cold. Made his mother crazy with worry until finally he held her while she cried and afterward they split a ham-and-butter sandwich. He wasn't sure meeting a sadder sack than him would help at all, but he did get up, he did do some push-ups and felt better for a minute. He showered, he shaved, he wished he had let his hair grow out just a little but he couldn't quite yet. Not yet. So he still looked the part. Jarhead.

She was smoking on his sister's porch when he pulled up. She wore black skinny jeans, and a big black baggy sweater. She pulled smoothly on the cigarette and turned her face to him when he stopped the car.

Shit. Fuck. She was drop-dead. She had dark long hair, upturned eyes black and lashy, a small nose and olive skin. The kind of girl you wouldn't even photo-brag about so as not to have your whole fucking unit masturbating to what was your own fantasy. So, this was his sister's game. Distract him by virtue of his dick. He laughed a little, finished the warmed can of beer he'd driven over with, played with his phone for a minute. Hoping his sister would come out, introduce them. Not make him find the words. She didn't and it was getting weird, he knew, how long he was sitting there, assuming she was watching him, waiting for him to get out. He took a breath, put his hand on the door handle and looked toward the porch.

She'd gone inside already. He wished he didn't feel so relieved and he thought other people wouldn't, other people just get out of their damn cars and introduce themselves, like the old him would have, but now he got out and walked up to his sister's perfect Victorian house. Little flowers planted in rows. Just like her dollhouse when they were kids. He loved that, he loved her, he would fight a million more times to keep this all exactly as it was right now for her. But he didn't think she knew that. And he didn't know if the two things, his fighting and her garden, really had anything to do with each other the way he had made himself believe for so long. She opened the door and rolled her eyes at him. You're late, she said. She had a full martini in one hand and held it away from her gray work dress, but that's okay, so is she. Esma, that's her name. She's always late, I guess. Want anything?

He started to open his mouth, to say, No, she was here, but then his sister started talking about her while getting him a beer from the fridge. Miller, in a bottle, his favorite. So Esma is my new assistant at work. She's good, creative. But she's a fucking disaster, she handed him the beer, So you know, I thought, Well, and she looked at him full in the face now, and let out a crooked smile. He sighed. She couldn't goad him, not since. She couldn't really piss him off. Cool, he said, to say something. And she sighed, Yeah, she said, cool, and took a drink. Sean's working late, she said, so we can order a pizza or something when Esma comes. Okay, he said, and brought his bottle to his cheek to rest his head.

Esma never came. Or never came back. They ordered a pizza

and his sister sent Esma a text after three martinis that said, You Are a Fucking Flake. But it's okay. See you tomorrow. She told him, I would call her a bitch or a ho, but you know, HR, and she rolled her eyes again.

She saw him in his car. Trying to avoid her. Meeting her. Looking at her. He was probably good looking, from what she could see. That All-American look. Soldier boy. But the thought of him, the potential of him and even his shyness, suddenly made her fucking tired. Like really, really, tired. So she jumped off the edge of the porch when he had his head down, cut through the neighbor's front yard, and walked home. She didn't really care if he saw her, but she didn't want to walk right in front of his car.

But on the next street over she berated herself for not at least meeting him. She knew he'd been in Iraq, had seen all sorts of gore and death. Had lost a close friend. Had never been the same.

But what did he know about her? That her father shot her mother and then himself in a hotel room three Christmases ago? Just because he'd lost all their money? That she was in Cabo and ducked into an internet café across from her hostel to check her email and read a message from the hotel manager who had found her on Facebook and messaged her in what she thought was some sicko's joke until her parents didn't answer her Skype calls even though it was Christmas? What did he think about that?

And how did his sister really see this playing out? Like the indie films she was always referencing at work? Like they'd get together, have some fun, but then really have to confront their issues and have some super cathartic scene where she'd be screaming and running into the ocean and he'd save her? Or they'd spend a night throwing water balloons off a hotel roof until one of them got on the ledge, maybe him, and this time it would be her turn to save him?

It was the question she knew plenty of people thought when they looked at her: How do you get over something like that? Is there a cure? Will she ever find a way?

Fuck no, she said to herself as she unlocked the door to her dingy bungalow, five blocks away and across the literal tracks from where she'd just been.

At least I can make eggs, she thought, and walked into the silent house, burrowing into its small darkness. Old walls like packed earth around her.

He left his sister asleep on the couch and got in his car and drove around for a while. At first he didn't know where he was going, taking turns around the neighborhood, then he thought he may be trying to get lost and then he realized he half-expected to see her, walking home still, under the dark trees, her cigarette aglow. He could introduce himself. Now, he could, in the dark, if they met by chance, after that many drinks. He would pull over and say, Hey, Aren't You Her? I am him. Do you need a ride somewhere?

But of course he didn't see her, and after not long he went home so he could get in bed and fall asleep before he sobered up.

The thing about extraordinary tragedy is that people always think you want to avoid it, forget it, brush it under the rug. They never mention "that thing that happened to you," or "what you must have gone through," unless they barely know you. A barkeep, for instance, knows what you need. To be asked about it, probed, he knows you want to press your face up against the glass behind which is the scene of your parents' murder-suicide. Or whatever happened. He knows you want to talk about them so much that they're in the room again, built back up by anecdote. He could also probably guess, that because her parents died the way they did, she now owns three guns. A shotgun, her father's weapon of choice, a nine-millimeter, and a thirty-eight. He could guess, maybe, that she'd taken a clean bullet and pressed its point hard into her chest right above her heart and imagined it exploding there. Imagined her mother's skin decimated. Tried to figure out once and for all if she knew it was coming, or if she refused to believe it until the bullet was well within her.

That morning he dreamt his worst dream. It had no real content he could hang on to, save for one woman, an Iraqi screaming, and a bloody child in her arms. The child's head half-gone. This was always the start of the dream, and then after it was just confusing, soldiers brushing past him, his panic rising, sand, wind, his mouth so so dry and he couldn't scream and couldn't move but knew he had to do both. He'd always wake up sweating, panting, and jump right out of bed.

He didn't know if the woman was a memory, or memories together. It was nothing he could place. Which made it everywhere he'd been, each microbattle, again. And again and again.

He finally met her the next week. His sister called and woke him up again and said, We, Esma and I, and she said Esma's name like it was a password, soft. We are on a deadline, and I was thinking maybe you could bring us lunch. Lunch, another password. Lunch? Yeah, sandwiches, from that place on ninth. Oh and Esma doesn't eat meat. Then she hung up. So he got up, skipped the push-ups, got in the shower, and let the water hit his chest until he felt less groggy. Turned the faucet to cold to be extra sure. Felt his blood recoil from his skin. Awake. He put on a plain gray t-shirt and jeans, didn't shave. Got three sandwiches, one veggie and two ham and cheese. Left the car outside the deli and walked the three blocks to his sister's office.

He walked into the open loft office, all exposed brick and standing desks, and caught Esma's eye right away. She didn't look away and this time neither did he. She put down her pencil, still wearing black, sultan pants actually, and approached him. Hey, she said, I'm Esma. Hey, he said, and held up the brown bag of sandwiches and chips like it was his name. Your sister is on the phone, she said, even though he could see his sister in her fishbowl, waving at him, holding a finger up, mouthing *one minute*. But come sit down, and she showed him to a corner of the office with black leather chairs and a glass table. He set the bag down and sat down, she stayed standing.

For a moment, he stared at the activity behind her, four or five people walking around, talking on the phone. It felt busy, this place. He wondered if he would like to be someplace busy. If he could be someplace busy.

He remembered then to look up at her, she was still standing with arms crossed. He was about to ask her if she liked working there, when she said, So, you were in Iraq? He expected that the minute she heard herself say it, Iraq, she would cringe, that she was one of those, but she didn't. So he smiled, Yeah, two tours.

His sister was off the phone now, Hey, she said and flopped down next to him. Damn, we are swamped. Did you meet Esma? Seriously, we are so behind. How did we get this behind? Is it my fault? I don't know, I don't know, but I'm starved. Thanks for bringing sandwiches, she lunged forward, what'd you get? She opened the bag, and pulled out the sandwiches, handing them out like gifts.

We met, he said, and remembered to look up and smile at Esma. She looked away, but something about this gesture wasn't unfriendly or shy, more like she didn't want to scare him, he thought.

Esma, his sister said, is a great artist, she's been whipping up some killer print ads. A piece of lettuce fell out of his sister's mouth and he chewed slowly.

And so they lunched together, and it was not all that awkward. Mostly they told him about the campaign they were working on, trying to sell Danish furniture. Print ads, TV, even radio (how do you not sound tacky trying to sell furniture on a radio ad? his sister asked, tucking a piece of ham into her lips). And he kept looking at her, and she at him, and his sister pretended not to notice (of course, she said when she called him later, two fucking good-looking people).

And so begins the montage. It is more than that, three or four months, but in a movie it would be a montage. Of them kissing in the rain, which they do for the first time a week after lunch on a *date walk* (her term), and which ends with them soaked and naked in her bed. Of her throwing a French fry at him at a late-night diner after seeing a bad movie. They do a lot of hanging out at her house, drinking wine slowly, making breakfast on weekends, and there's no minigolf or roller-coasters but still you can frame it like a montage. With them half-dressed or undressed most of the time. A beautiful display of the American Romantic Comedy that felt about as far away as possible for him just a year earlier.

And if it was a montage it would end here: the music would fade as the camera zoomed in on them sleeping peacefully in her bed, their beautiful bodies half-draped in a paisley sheet. And then. UP. UP.

He was up. He was already on his feet. Sweating, shaking, trying to catch his breath. Had he stopped breathing in his sleep? Had he knocked over her lamp? She was up, now too, What, what? Jesus, did you hear something?

And there it was. The peace over. The dream again. He had

had it throughout the montage but a quieter version. The woman without the child, the woman waving, his buddies' voices but not the panic. But it had come back.

He sat back down on the bed, tried to catch his breath.

The woman, the child with the destroyed head, a broken pomegranate with a doll's mouth. And she had looked up from her screaming. And she was Esma. His beautiful, dark-featured Esma. How had he never noticed this before?

She looked fucking A-rab.

She reached her hand across the bed and lay her palm flat across his panting back.

It wasn't voluntary, but he winced and slammed the slowing montage into his past.

Jesus, she said, you okay?

He couldn't get out of there fast enough, not to mention say what he knew he could say, that it was a dream, a recurring dream, that they are a common symptom of vets with PTSD. Could say, but couldn't.

He got up, pulled on his clothes, and left.

Outside in the blue-gray dawn he ran home. He felt better as soon as the air got into his lungs, he felt stronger than the image. Just a dream. A stupid fucking dream. But his relief was short-lived. Fuck. He'd really fucked up. Totally freaked. Showed her the monster he'd managed to hide so far. He should run back.

He should go get coffee, breakfast, bring it to her, apologize. But he couldn't. It was that frozen space, the skin-splitting stage, he felt sick, and got home just in time to puke in his mom's kitchen sink.

He curled up in bed and it started to rain outside. He let all of his memories of Iraq come back, he went over them again and again, the worst ones first. The worst one. His friend, Wiley, walking there on the road in front of him. Telling a dirty joke and half-turned toward him and then gone. The world became sound. He could see nothing but heard through his eyes. Heard dust and an arm and maybe a tongue in the sand. His sight came back and he saw first thing his scream a windstorm. Wiley lost in it. Again. Again and again. He puked twice more. His mother came in and said, A bug. She went to the pharmacy to buy Pedialyte and saltines. He stayed in bed shaking.

Esma called three times that day, but he didn't call her back. The next day his sister called. He didn't answer. It was like he had remembered not to be happy. That he didn't deserve it. Other friends hadn't made it. Children hadn't made it.

His sister called him the next day and yelled at him for fifteen minutes. He hadn't said a word back other than *I know*, and finally she hung up. He called his buddy with the dog but hung up after it started ringing.

The third day his truck was plastered in "Support Our Troops" stickers. Pressed right onto the paint. She knew how much he hated those yellow ribbons. Felt they were a joke. He'd never let his mom put one on her Honda Civic. She'd bought one, right before he left for his second tour, and shown it to him with delight. So everyone knows, she said, and thinks about you all. But he'd shaken his head at her, No, he said. Everybody sees those and doesn't think about us. That's the worst part.

He didn't take a single one off before he drove to her place. People honked and waved at him with geeky smiles at stoplights. Why? Did they know he was a vet now? Did they think he was just feeling extra patriotic? He parked in her driveway and turned the car off. His head hurt and he pressed his forehead as hard as he could into the steering wheel. Thought about driving back home. He was so tired. But then she was there, opening his door.

What the fuck? she said it angrily at first and then softer. What the fuck as she pulled herself into his lap and put her arms around his neck. She smelled sour, like she hadn't showered since he'd left her bed forty-eight hours earlier. It wasn't a bad smell though and he buried his face in her hair.

They went from the truck to the bed and then she fixed them eggs and Clamato and beer. Sorry about your truck, she said.

And then she told him. She told him about the Facebook message, how she tried her parents and couldn't get through, first on Skype and then by phone, how she googled *murder-suicide* and the hotel her parents were staying at and then waited while the slowest internet connection in the world finally pulled up the news story. How she was already on a plane home, her bags left at the hostel, by the time the detective tracked her down. She told him the scene as she imagined it. The medical examiner's office. The case file, she told him about how she had gone over it and over it in her head. Was she just shocked or was there a possibility that they got it wrong? There were small details that seemed off. A glass on the floor in the corner. Why? She had for a month kept a glass in the corner of her bedroom, rolled on its side, just in case she saw it one day and suddenly knew why the other one had been there. But then one morning she looked up and there was a giant spider in there. A daddy longlegs. It was so easy it was depressing, she tipped the glass so it was upside down and he was caught. She left him there and the next day he was dead, long legs folded in.

He asked, what do you think happened, really?

She grabbed her head, she looked tired. Tired like him. I won't ever know, she said. Probably just what they say.

Later, she pulled up the rug that lay next to her bed and told him to get up and lie on the floor by the bed. Right on the carpet. She turned him on his side and took his top arm and pinned it slightly behind him, his legs in a scissors pattern. Then she got a black marker out of her bedside table and took off the lid. It should be white, she said, but then we couldn't see it. The carpet was beige. She edged the marker along his spine and down the front of his bottom leg. She was drawing an outline of his body. Like a murder scene. Like he was her father. But she didn't say this. Her hand lightly tickled as it silhouetted his naked body and he did not to want to get an erection so he closed his eyes, took a deep breath. She slipped around his ankle and he felt the felt tip of the marker on his skin. Shit, she said, and took her thumb, licked it, and smudged the ink off his bone before she continued. He tried to imagine death this way. One body. Intact. And time. Attention paid. Movement, precision, care, around each fragment of the murder. He said it before he thought it.

Your dad was a lucky man.

His stomach turned as he heard it and her hand paused in the drawing, she was almost to the back of his neck. But then she kept drawing.

I don't know, she said. I don't know any more what he was. What they were.

I just meant, he said, but he stopped. He didn't know how to explain. But was glad to know it, to think it. That her parents' bodies had been cared for.

It couldn't have been all about money, he said.

She stopped drawing and looked at him like he'd slapped her.

No, she said, no. I know.

He pulled her down on top of him to his chest. She curled into him.

He wanted, then, to tell her about the woman and the child. But he didn't. Not for weeks.

In the hours he was gone, after she had put the stickers on his car, she had googled images of the Iraq War. *Have you done this?* She threw up within fifteen minutes. There are pictures of people with the lower half of their bodies gone. Just gone. Red spaghetti messes where their torsos should be. Caved in heads. Skulls blown apart. Legs lying in the middle of the road. And the bodies of children. Lined up on the curb. Soldiers cradling dead toddlers with confused looks on their faces, as if they were wondering how their own child got in the middle of this? As if they are just going to get up, take this still child in her pink t-shirt and jeans and carry her home, put her in bed, tuck her in, and kiss her goodnight.

She didn't ever tell him she did this, but a few weeks later his sister gently touched her arm at work and asked her how she thought he was doing, you know, with all *that*. Those images came back to her and suddenly she wanted to throw her coffee in her face. His sister always talked about him like he just couldn't fucking get it together, like he was a kid that failed to launch rather than a war vet. So she looked at her and told her, He's fucking fine, and then she apologized, felt the need to explain and so ended up telling her about the photos. Told her she thought she might have fucking PTSD just from the internet.

She didn't tell her that she wished she had seen a picture of her parents' bodies. That she knows there has to be one. That one day she'll get the courage to ask the detective to see it.

She didn't tell her that she doesn't see how he'll ever be able to be a father. Not after that place. Those kids.

And she didn't tell her that even though she's pregnant, she doesn't think she could be a mother either. She couldn't imagine waking from nightmares to nurse a child.

His sister called him one weeknight crying. He could tell she'd had a few drinks. She told him she'd been looking at photos of the war online, how she had never done that before and now she's really fucking sorry. Sorry that she looked, sorry that he was there, that he went through that. He didn't know what to say. He had his own sick collection of photos, so did his buddy with the dog, but he actually hadn't done the google thing. Oh god, his sister said, suddenly panicked, oh god, well if you haven't then don't. She seemed to sober up, and blew her nose. Seriously, don't, I don't know about PTSD but that seems like a bad idea. Promise me you won't.

He promised but he was on the computer fifteen minutes later. The photos he found at first were mild, nothing new. His heartbeat didn't quicken. In fact, he found himself looking through them hoping to see someone he knew, or a place he went to.

And that's when he found it. The woman, her face an open-mouth scream. The child, head half-blown.

It wasn't a dream then.

At the end of the week he went over again to her little bungalow with old, crooked wood floors and dark heavy curtains and they drank wine. She had a glass and a half before she thought that maybe she shouldn't. He didn't notice she didn't finish her second glass, but she noticed he was more talkative than usual, telling her stories about funny things that happened in training. He finished the bottle of wine for them both, finally said he was getting sleepy.

Me, too, she said, but when she turned off the light she lay awake for a long time. She was thinking that maybe tomorrow she would tell him and they could figure out what to do together. She shut her eyes and tried not to picture her mother's face, tried not think about how excited she would have been about a baby. Tried not to think in red and useless circles. Tried not to think about what a shitty world it was. The backs of her eyes felt dry by the time she didn't remember falling asleep.

So the next morning he is out on her back patio with its grassy cracks, having toast with jam for breakfast in the morning sun. Nothing fancy, she says. He is feeling better than he has in a while so he decides to tell her. About the dream.

It never goes that well, telling people dreams. There's this time and weird noncorrelational dimensionality to them. How he could see the woman and child as from afar but then for a brief moment as from within. How the panic that he couldn't move was also a panic that his legs were gone. The sand. The child.

As he speaks, she seems to listen quietly, her hands clenched in her lap. She is getting ready to say, I'm sorry, to say the quiet words that he knows that she knows are meaningless. What does one say to that kind of tragedy? They know. (The bartender, he knows.) But then his tone shifts. But then, he says, my sister calls me the other night.

His face was warmer now, and she tilted forward a little. His fucking sister, was her first thought, but then she saw he was laughing.

Suddenly, then, he was telling a joke: God knows why, but she's been looking at photos of the war online. She's fucking upset, and tells me not to look but of course I do. And I'm going through these photos, which aren't that bad, and actually looking to see if any of my buddies are in them, and what do I see?

The fucking woman! He slapped his knee and his voice was louder than she had ever heard it. Like he was just realizing it at that moment, he said, So all these years I've been having this same nightmare, this same image, and it wasn't a fucking memory, he says, it was a photo. It was all over the fucking place, on the fucking cover of *Time* magazine. He was practically shouting when he got to the punch line, when he said he looked it up and the photo was taken in Mosul, said he'd never even been there, and then he looked at her and grinned. Shrugged like, isn't life the darndest? Took a giant bite of his toast. It was like she was watching his heart balloon out, rise up, and float away while she was weighted down by the soft egg in her abdomen.

Her doctor had told her it was the size of a raisin earlier that week, but it felt much heavier.

A stone.

He wipes the crumbs off his mouth, and looks at her. She looks like she might be sick, and he notices she's only had one bite of toast. Shit, he says, was that too much? That image, at breakfast? Fuck, I didn't even think about it. She shakes her head, No, she says, I just need a cigarette. She pulls a pack and lighter from behind a dead plant on the windowsill. Her hands shake as she pulls one from the pack and lights it.

I mean, yeah, he says, it's still a bummer about that kid. But it's not something I saw that I couldn't have seen in an airport gift shop, you know?

She knew she should tell him. She should tell him what worried her most. Or what haunted her most, how she was up often in the night while others slept, cataloguing her interactions with her father over her lifetime. How she had tried to figure out: if she hadn't decided to head to Cabo, had decided to go to San Diego with them, would he have killed her too? Spared her? She knew she should have told him this, or about the pregnancy, or anything, but her tongue felt like a gag stuffed in her mouth. Her throat fibrous and dry.

The sun too bright.

He realizes he hasn't seen her smoke for a while but now he enjoys it. That elegance from the first night he saw her on his sister's porch. He feels so different now, like a different person. He feels light, maybe like his old self. But also like his new self, one that could take care of her. He feels like they could be a normal, happy couple, that maybe he could have all those things he would have by now if he'd never gone. He doesn't think about if he'll have more dark days, he knows he will, but now, he thinks, he could have this kind of day too. A good day. A light day.

She exhaled smoke into the morning sun and remembered a time when she was little and she let a large splinter fester in her palm, afraid of the pain of removing it. By the time she showed her father, it was red and pussing. He was furious and lectured her about self-care, but then he was ever so gentle as he cut and squeezed around the splinter, getting out every last bit when it broke apart, the wood softened by her blood. He made her soak her hand for an hour and checked it three more times to be sure he'd gotten it all.

She'd always thought of this moment as love, but now it reminded her of his inability to leave anything behind. An obsession with perfection.

And it was like that way with everything: nothing in her past read the same, it was all scrambled. Silent. No future would be how she once thought it would.

He knows he can have more good days, can work at it, maybe get a dog. Maybe an apartment of his own, a job at the VA. He eyes her uneaten toast, suddenly ravenous.

She had thought maybe, for a minute, she had thought maybe. But now she thought, it will crush me, it's *that* heavy, and she knew it as soon as he turned to her, again with that grin, and said, for the first time ever,

So, what do you want to do today?

Prelingual

S he said to me, "We are at a crossroads." She was leaning forward, jeweled hands clasped together professionally. Her head was tilted and I thought about two barren and uncertain roads stretching their whole lives until one day they discovered they crossed.

"No," I told her, "I don't think so." Though I did know what she meant. It was getting difficult to tell who was which gender between us. I told her, "Well, you may be right. I can't tell your gender anymore."

"I am a man," she said, with confidence.

"That's exactly what I mean," I told her.

She was my psychoanalyst and it was Tuesday. We had recently excavated through the junior high years but around 1992 we hit rock. It seemed impenetrable, even for a Tuesday. But I never for a minute feared I was wasting my money. Such was *my* confidence.

She said to me, "Things have come to a head." She had her pencil in hand and was tapping it lightly on her small yellow notepad. I knew but didn't tell her that this was never going to get us to 1991.

"Pumpkin," I said.

"What?"

"You said head, I said pumpkin. First thing that came to mind."

"No, no," she said, "this isn't free association."

"Oh," I said, trying not to look discouraged.

She raised her pencil to her teeth as if to chew it, but stopped herself.

"But," I tried, "if you think about it, it makes sense pumpkin, head. Pumpkin heads."

"But it's April." She sighed. I sensed she was becoming frustrated so I opened my lunch bag and took out a pear. It was only barely bruised. I set it on her desk.

She stared at it for a moment. She said, "Why don't you tell me again about that time you saw the baby?"

"My sister's baby?" I asked.

She shrugged, so I continued.

"I saw it. I saw it and saw it for a half hour while my sister talked. Things were going well."

"And then what happened?"

"I got up to leave. I had to be at a meeting. I went to hug the baby. But it was too small. Too small to hug. My sister said, What are you doing? You are going to crush my baby. So I had to squeeze its tiny palm with my index finger and thumb. It felt inadequate, as a gesture, as a goodbye, and even the word *goodbye* didn't seem quite enough when the baby finally released her grip on my finger. Then I left, wondering, is it ever enough?"

"And?" She said. Tapping her pencil on her chin, eyeing the pear.

"That's when we realized I am terrified of smallness. I think you called it—the essence of vulnerability? Yes, that was it."

"Was it smallness, though, was it?" She reached over to grab the pear, peeling off the fruit sticker tenderly, like it was a Band-Aid on a child's arm.

"Yes," I said confidently. "We decided that smallness is generally crushing."

She took a bite and nodded, waiting for me to say more. I did not. If not smallness, what, then? Softness? But I did not ask this, afraid of her disapproval.

"What meeting did tou thave?" she asked, biting into the pear.

"What do you mean what meeting?"

"The one you had to leave the baby to go to."

"Oh there was no meeting, that is just a saying. A cliché."

"No." She swallowed pear. "It's not." She sighed.

"Oh, well then maybe I was coming here."

"This is not a meeting. It's an appointment." This time when she bit into the pear, its juice ran down her chin in a clear trickle. She didn't bother to wipe it and I thought: wow. I thought: reckless. I was impressed.

"An appointment," I repeated, smiling. "Got it."

She finished her pear in silence and threw it over her shoulder. I saw for the first time that there was a garden behind her chair, lining the back wall of her office. A small wild growth. It must have just sprung up.

She said to me, "You only live once." She was wiping her mouth, taking off her glasses and I thought, well, okay, fine.

"That's new," I said, and pointed to the wall of plants.

"No, it's not. You are only noticing it now because we've exhausted all other possibilities."

"Is 1991 in there?" I asked.

"You tell me, pumpkin head," she was slouching in her chair now, arms hanging slack off the sides and I thought perhaps maybe she was right about her gender.

I stood up and walked to the edge of the garden, which was a forest now. It was thick and dark in there and clearly not a metaphor for my past.

"It's not," I sighed with relief. "Nope, no early years in there."

"Shit," she said. She/he swiveled her chair around. She/he seemed completely at her wit's end. She had ruffled hair now, and a moony look in her eyes. A muted glint. I wanted to say: You look like a drunk wolf. But I already felt bad enough. Here he/she was, coming undone right before my childhood.

Here we were, together, only living once.

So I said, "No, I take that back," I took a breath and stepped from the carpet onto the cakey, needled ground. "There may be something here."

There was a pause. She/he cleared her throat, I sensed a sitting-up-straight happening behind me.

"What do you see?" I could hear the pencil being taken up. The date and Tuesday no doubt being written down.

"Well," I had to be careful. She would know I was faking if I wasn't careful. I had to think. "Well," I had to think, think. I took another step in. I could hear the forest making room for me. Did I actually remember anything from that string of years?

"Baseball," I said. "There was a baseball and it was falling at me and it was small but grew bigger as it fell, and I looked up at it and noticed the sky was the color of milk."

I didn't have time to wonder if this last detail was too over-the-top because all I heard was *keep going*, only she sounded far away now because I had begun to walk into the musky thick air of the forest, looking for a way out, a clearing, a place where two roads might actually be in the act of discovering they crossed.

"It hit me," I concluded, and vanished without saying goodbye into a space too large to be contained in my small form.

Fucking Aztecs

We should have known it wasn't going to be that simple, the Aztecs were always pulling shit like this, since the day they showed up in Colhuacan. We even had a saying we whispered on hot market days when they came to trade: to trust an Aztec, well, you might as well ask the cactus to be smooth. But we had all been living in proximity and relative peace for a while and then they reached out to us, asked us over and the offer sounded so good, you know? They asked us to a dinner, a party in honor of Achitometl's daughter, who was now a goddess married to their favorite god. They said they would have a feast, celebrate our two peoples. They said we could see their temple. They said it would be a nice evening and it sounded nice. I mean, what could go wrong?

Apparently, everything.

First we should have put two and two together. How *does* a woman marry a god? Achitometl was like a blushing *ahuiani* when they asked him, and shoved his little *cihuāpil* right out the door without asking for the details. The nitty-gritty. Because, in hindsight, it seems obvious that she couldn't stay in her form and marry a god. She'd have to be something else, right? You got to hand it to the

Aztecs for that anyway. Counting on us never to know the right questions to ask.

They'd always been a step ahead of us. Achitometl actually relied for a while on this idea his wacko right-hand man, Neza told him: Hang tight, he told us all as they encroached upon our land, took over the lakefront, began marrying our women. I have foreseen that the vipers and lizards will drive them out.

But fucking Aztecs. They just ate the reptilian evil that had kept the rest of us from living near the water, and seemed all the better for it. And we knew, had heard tell, not to start shit with them even if we did outnumber them. That they got all giddy for war. Killing and blood was their thing, so they really had nothing to lose once you got into it with them. And we all know that kid in a fight. It doesn't matter how small he is, he's terrifying.

And still, there was something seductive about them. They had these eyes like cats, and the women wore their hair braided with ribbons on festival days. When they fucked up, or said something stupid, they slit their own tongues in half, and the healed lingual wounds made them look like they had turned into the snakes they had eaten. They had this dreamy quality about them, too.

They were fucking poets.

Sure they murdered all the time, their slaves, mostly. But it was all with pure intentions. Blood and body wasn't too . . . I don't know how to put it, not that they didn't think it was delicate, because they did what they did with precision and pomp. They just didn't flinch. They were that sure of themselves. And it was sexy.

What can I say? The Aztecs were like your oldest brother's coolest friend, so even though we knew better—because we fucking knew better—when they invited us to a party, we went with our tongues hanging out.

Achitometl sent word out eight days before, saying we'd all been asked to a feast in honor of his daughter, the newly coronated Aztec goddess, wife of Huitzilopochtli. He was all puffed with pride and insisted we get on our best loincloths and join him. And so for those few days it was all anyone talked about: the feast. We all secretly nursed a perverse hope we might see one of their famous sacrifices, and we each brought something from our pile of special.

My own pile consisted of an eagle feather, a raven feather, three cacao beans, a half-burnt piece of paper, a dried prickly pear flower, and a scrap of tin shaped like fish tail.

I decided on the raven feather. I know I know, the more patriotic Colhuacan would have brought the eagle feather. But I had just found it. And I meant to give it to Ayauhcihuatl on our next walk. The walk. So the raven feather it was.

The Aztecs had a thing about architecture. Their builder really did have a good eye, and a fine sense of geometry. Some among us said that's why they were consenting to going to the feast: to see the new temple. Like they were fucking cultural attachés who simply had to see the latest in Mesoamerican art. But I knew that they, too, held high hopes for a sacrifice.

I know what you are thinking. That we get sacrificed. That we get invited to dinner and What Do You Know? we are the dinner.

But the Aztecs are too fucking head-in-the-clouds for that shit. It's not like they do shit for the hell of it. It may appear all laissez-faire later on in history, but it was systematic. The hearts cut out of the sacrificial victims? Not just a parlor trick. They really think that the heart is a fragment of the sun trapped in the body.

It must be freed so it can return. The debt paid.

No, what happened is this. We went, and it was nice. It was really fucking nice. Achitometl, fat and balding, led us waddling to their temple, which did not disappoint the cultural attachés. It was a pyramid of adobe stairs, and inside it was cavernous and cool and closed above us like a mountain. In the half-dark, they fed us their finest: maize and beans the color of bone, with bowls of black chocolatl, which made us all feel pleasantly buzzed. We ate, and then we rested back on lusty rugs of jaguar skin. Achitometl's daughter was nowhere in sight, but that seemed fitting for a goddess, to make some late and ceremonial entrance. There was a feeling that they were watching us—and that we were watching them, the way the room was set up, with them on one side and us on the other. But overall, it was pretty fucking relaxing.

Then the High Priest, or one of them, with an elaborate diadem and gold nose plugs and lip rings and his lower arms plated in gold, came to Achitometl and nodded at him. A younger priest stood behind him, dressed as an ocelot, and asked Achitometl if he'd like to see his daughter, in the inner temple. Achitometl jumped up and brushed his greasy hands on his loincloth. He gathered what he had brought to offer, a small cage of kitchen quail, a bundle of orange dahlias and twigs of incense. We watched as he approached the altar at the door of the inner temple. He looked at the High

Priest, who gave a slight nod, then he set the cage on the floor and gently took out a quail who made no sound as he took his knife from his belt and slit its throat, opening it upon the altar so that the blood spilt out before plucking a few flower heads off, sticking them in the dead bird's mouth, and placing it onto the altar. He ended by scattering incense atop. He looked back at the High Priest, obviously pleased with himself, but the High Priest was a hard man to read. He really only wore one expression, and so committed the same small nod he had a moment ago.

We all watched this in silence, and were silent when they took Achitometl back into the inner temple to see his daughter. He disappeared through an opening in the stone and we waited.

The chocolatl was done by then, and we all watched for his return in a kind of drunken alertness. The room was growing darker, the fires dimmer. As I stared at the opening, waiting, my eyes seemed not to adjust but to become blinder in the dark, and in the flickers of firelight I thought I saw movement, his return, several times. I fingered the hairs of the feather in my lap. I wondered which was blacker, my feather, or the jaguar's fur. I thought perhaps my feather, that because the jaguar was so black, it might actually bounce off its own blackness and become lighter. I wasn't sure when we would all give our offerings, and thought maybe Achitometl would come back with his daughter and then we'd have some kind of to-do.

It was hard to say how long he was gone. We began to grow fidgety. We hadn't yet seen a sacrifice, and now the anticipation of blood seemed like bad karma on our part. We had our flint knives on our belts and felt their weight become heavier in the thickening temple air. Our people began to shift around, a few sat up, but none dared stand.

The Aztecs, on the opposite end of the room, did not fidget. They sat straight and still and the whites of their almond eyes shone on us. It was a little creepy. The uncanniest thing is that when I think back on it—now that I know what was happening in that room, that Achitometl was struggling to see just like us, until he saw what they had done—I really couldn't tell you if the Aztecs in the room with us knew or not. If they thought, like us, that their goddess might be making an appearance at any moment, or if they knew that she had been killed and that presently a young priest was dressed in her skin, waiting for Achitometl to kill the rest of his quails so that he could step into the light and show himself. They had no expressions, no betraying smirks, not even any energy anticipating one thing or the other. So it's like they didn't know they were about to go to war, or did know but had always known since before the dawn of their time and either way left them poised with a stifling calm, so sophisticated that it seemed more animal than human.

In the end we heard him before we saw him. He was yelling, You assholes! And I remember thinking: oh shit, they've made his daughter into a man-eater. But then he ran into the great room, mouth open, tongue out, wild eyes, knife and hatchet one in each hand, the look on his face like a torn-up tree. Come on, he yelled to us, and we got up, but slowly, waking from the dream of waiting in the quiet nest of stone. Come on! he yelled again, They killed her! His voice was high: they dressed a man in her skin and I made sacrifices to this beast before I could see . . . and here he broke down. He was a total wreck, poor guy, but we were all awake now and on our feet and so Neza finished the decree for him in Nahuatl: Death and destruction to men so evil with such vile customs. Let not a trace of their memory remain.[1]

The Aztecs in the room had not moved at all, they had watched this from their sea of tranquility. Unfazed, even, when we took our knives and hatchets out and bared our teeth. Which we did, we drew our weapons in the lowlight and went at them. I managed to bury my raven feather deep within by belt for safekeeping before raising my own blade.

We killed several of them right there in the dark belly of their temple. I myself felt a few soft insides with my knife. The battle moved outside and we drove the Aztecs back toward the lake, until we were fighting them knee-deep in water when the sky ripened with dawn. We had backup from Colhuacan by then, and basically had them surrounded. They stood waist-deep in water and we on the shore. This standoff lasted until the next morning.

Then something happened—I think they made a break for it, and I think we sort of let them, too tired ourselves of guarding them on the buggy lake beach when they threw the few spears they had left at our men and all of them, women and children too, ran right out of the water, through us and away.

Just like that, gone.

So that was the end of our time in proximity to the Aztecs, and though we talk shit about them, the serpent eaters' blood still runs among us: the cat-slanted eyes, the braids our women wear now, the red berries of the new cacao trees.

---

1. According to Fray Diego Duran, a sixteenth-century writer who studied the Aztecs, these were the words spoken by Achitometl on this occasion.

My raven feather was stiff with dried blood when I pulled it out of my belt that morning, and I've kept it through the years. Sometimes at night, I roll the quill between two fingers and watch the blackness of the bird flicker in and out of the firelight and I remember sitting in the dark with them, the Aztecs, the whites of their cat eyes, their deafening calm, as if they were waiting always and forever for the moment when we would finally understand and free them from us. I drop the feather when this image comes, but not before I start to feel the warmth of my heart inside my chest, and know it for what it really is:

a hot, beating piece of sun whose time inside my body is dull, but gratefully brief.

Time Just Isn't That Simple

When the kids come by with their research reports, I start by telling them about the excruciatingly long car ride to school. How my family carpooled with a pack of miscreants, one of whom was sickly. I like to use words like *miscreants* and *sickly* to evoke the otherness of that time for them. I tell them too about the television chimpanzee in those years, how smart she was and yet unable to master the art of macramé. They are always amazed, these children, when I tell them there was no Child Protective Services, and that computers were bigger than microwaves.

If they come by and I don't feel like talking, they ask for some spare change. They tell me they like to throw coins at the door of the artist down the street, So he won't kill himself for God's sake, they say.

Sometimes when they come by they have specific questions. They stand with hands on their child hips on my stoop and want to know if I had ever had unprotected sex. I tell them I don't remember. Then they ask a number of questions concerning my childhood chores, allowance, and birthday parties. They seem to be trying to decide if it was better to be a kid when I was a kid, then, or better to be a kid when they are kids, now. But when I really begin to sift back through the years for them and tell them about the free milk at school, they begin to grow restless. Finally, exasperated, they ask what people did for fun.

So I invite them in, sit them down, pour out some lemonade and decide to tell them about the parties. My parents used to have these parties in the summer, I tell them, and there'd always be cola and cherry soda and those nights would go late late.

How late? They ask. There are four of them this day.

Orange late, I tell them. Which they understand in terms of Homeland Security, and I in old streetlights, dreary florescent triangles.

I tell them, My parents' friends would come over and send their kids down to the basement, where I would be waiting with pretzel sticks and goldfish and Uno and movies recorded off the television. The mothers would go to the kitchen, and the fathers, who were all half-fathers, would go out back to the patio to drink beer.

Of course, these kids say, nodding their heads because their own dads in fact drink beer on their own patios. This is timeless. Though they are typing *goldfish*, *Uno*, and *half-fathers* into their search engines. I tell them to put the contrivances away and give them a bowl of dry beans to fondle, which is both the only way they can listen, and when they know I mean to tell a story.

The fathers were all half-fathers because they stopped at the waist, either because they had no legs like my dad, had legs too wounded to use, or had gotten too large, their thighs like baby whales. So they had chairs or motorized carts or crutches and this was because of the things fathers did back then, which was go to war, have industrial accidents, or get disability for inadvertent largeness.

The only one of the fathers who was not a half man was my dad's high-school friend Danny. Danny had a glass eye, so he'd been kept from the army and the other things that halved you.

He had to be a lawyer instead, which came in handy when the neighbor kids' dad was crushed by a steel beam at work that took off his left hand and papered his legs for good. Danny saw to it that they got a hot tub and a big screen and college funds and lots of other things.

I liked Danny because at one of these parties I ran outside barefoot—raiding the patio for father fondles and hair-tugs, half-empty beers, and other tokens of that foreign love—and I asked Danny if I could look at his eye. Danny squinted hard and out it popped. It was round and lovely like a misshapen jawbreaker with a blue center. I fingered it carefully, it was just a little wet on one side. The eye felt strange in my hand, and as I reached to give it back to Danny, it dropped onto the cement and rolled under the table. I crawled down and got it and it wasn't broken or even cracked, which I thought might be lucky, so I ran to the hose to wash it off but when I came back Danny told me to keep it.

Really? the kids ask, gripping their fistfuls of pinto beans now, imagining probably, the holding of an eye.

Yes, really. I ran to show my older brother the prize and we put it in a little soap dish on our special-collection shelf alongside the sand dollar our aunt had sent us, the thin French fry–shaped bone we'd found, and the crooked line of our baby teeth. But the next day when I showed my mother our new addition, she bristled and told me I had to take it back, that Danny was probably drunk when he gave it to me. So I had to wrap it in a bunch of paper napkins and then put it in a sock and tie the sock to my handlebars and bike over to Danny's house, which I'd been to with my dad and which was not far. Danny's yard was parch dry but his porch looked nice and bare swept, with an empty swing. When I knocked on the door and no one answered I swung for a while and looked at the neighborhood, which was made up of clean little box houses like Danny's, some with kids' toys in the yard and one with a dog chained to a tree. It was an old spotted dog and it was sleeping. I watched the street for a while, and I even covered one eye so I could see it like Danny. When I got bored I knocked again and Danny came to the door with a patch like a pirate on his face, even though his socket wasn't gross or anything, just black like the mouth of a cave. He said, Hey kid, what is it? So I slowly unwrapped his eye and held it out to him, but he looked in my palm and it seemed to gross him out. Like it wasn't his. He looked away, toward the old dog and told me to go on and take it, that really it irritated his eyehole, never quite fit right, and then he looked back at me and told me that he wanted me to have it. I held it out again, but he shook his head and I thought he looked sad, so I asked him if he wanted to swing with me on his porch and he said no, he had some work to do.

He's like the artist, the kids whisper, echoing exactlys until I give them a look and go on.

Well then I told Danny thank you and I said, I like your patch. And he nodded and closed the door. I wrapped the eye back up and put it back in my sock and biked home. But I didn't put Danny's eye back on our shelf, or tell my mother I had it, instead I wrapped it in a silk handkerchief my grandmother had given me and put it in my underwear drawer so that I wouldn't lose it.

Do you still have it? they ask, stopping their hands in the bean noise.

No, but those nights were magical, I tell them. The mothers would be in heels and smell like fancy department stores and I would watch them sometimes from the top of the basement stairs. Their skirts would look like lampshades floating around the kitchen, glasses would be clinking and their laughter was rich and deep like it used to be when women really smoked. Sometimes if these parties went more late late than even usual, the mothers would finish the dishes and then began slow dancing together in the kitchen. They missed dancing, they said, the half-fathers couldn't stand close to them, sway with them, and I remember watching my mother and our neighbor Janet holding each other tight, swaying like a buoy. My mother's face was so peaceful then, like a bowl of quiet milk.

And that, I tell them as they grip and grip, curling their feet against the slowness of my story, is how I came to later invent the dancing machine.

This gets them. They drop beans like hail into the bowl. What is a dancing machine? they sing at me in round.

Listen, I say. Shortly after I saw my mother with her quiet milk face, I decided I had to see it again. So, on a regular night with no party, I got my mother to sit on my father's leg stumps and hold him and I rocked his chair back and forth to a slow jazz record. But my father's legs started to hurt because of his lack of circulation and my mom's knees had to hang over the arm of the chair and then she was taller than him, and couldn't put her head on his chest and lose herself. My mother told me, It's not working and got up and went to watch TV and my father shrugged and went off to smoke. I stood there listening to Billie Holiday by myself and felt like crying. That's when I first thought I would marry me a man like Danny, who I was sure could dance just fine, I tell them.

Did you? they ask. Did your husband have a glass eye too?

No, I tell them, and *hush*.

My mother's milk face got put away then and it wasn't until almost a decade later when the idea for the harness came to me. My brother and I were in high school and we wanted to do something real nice for Mother's Day because it turned out our mother was sick, and even though she got better later, after all her hair fell out, we thought maybe it was going to be our last chance. So I told my brother about the dancing I'd seen all those years ago in the kitchen and had never forgotten and we got the idea that if we could hang my dad up somehow, suspend him to standing, they could dance. So we decided to convert the rope swing tied to the weeping willow out back into a dancing machine.

Then we got serious, I tell them. To invent something, one must get serious.

They nod. This will make a great report, they whisper.

My brother and I went out to the old swing, first I climbed on, then he, two loops below me. We were testing, I tell them, its weight-bearing abilities. We borrowed a chest harness from our neighbor Luke, who had everything because he had once wanted to be a Navy Seal, and we slung it up right according to knots we looked up in a book at the school library. We gave it a test run, my brother clipped in, knees bent so he'd hang like my father would, and I held him and we pretended to dance. She'll have to lead, my brother said, and I unclipped him.

On the big night, I tell them, we hauled a card table out to the yard and put some candles on it, they were apple-cinnamon scented because that's all we could find around the house. Then we told my dad the plan and he said, Well, fine, if you think she'll like it, and I told him to put on some cologne, because he'd be dancing with his wife for the first time in years. He said he'd go clean up and wheeled away. Then we got the boom box out, plugged it in with an extension cord coming out of my bedroom window, and put it on the card table.

What is a boom box? the smallest kid asks, sucking the beans that have found their way into her mouth.

A stereo. I'd made a mix of Billie Holiday, Al Green, Ella Fitzgerald, and some of my own favorites like Cyndi Lauper's "Time After Time." These are musicians who sang good love songs then. When evening came we told Mother her surprise was ready and she best clean up. She had her hair still then, but was really very tired because she'd had a big surgery not too long before where they took out most of her insides, or at least that's how it looked to us, like she'd been sucked empty. It took her a long time to put on a skirt and a blouse. While we waited my father wheeled outside, all fresh shaven and hair combed. He looked at the harness and shook his head. Damn kids, he said.

The artist says that, two of these kids say almost at once.

When mother appeared out of the bedroom she looked shiny, and I felt glad she'd put some cream or makeup on or something. You look beautiful, I said. You have to stop a minute, and I stood her behind the back-door screen and put the silk handkerchief, borrowed from Danny's eye for the occasion, around her eyes. Wait here, I told her and I went to help my brother with my father. He smelled like cloves as my brother picked him up out of the chair and held him while I fastened the harness to his broad arms, across his chest, and cinched it against his heart. Might as well be a meat hook, my father said. But he smiled. We lit candles and the drooping willow leaves shone like a curtain in an old painting. I hit play on the tape deck (boom box) and then my brother and I went to lead my mother outside. We were so careful with her between us.

When we got her to my father's arms, she started and my father laughed. You forgot I was taller than you, didn't you? he said and she took off the blindfold. I said, Dance, dance! The song "You Can't Take That Away from Me" was playing, and sure enough they began to sway, my mom smiling big, and I thought she was happy but I did not yet see the milk face.

The children stop touching the beans altogether. Was the dancing machine invented for nothing? they ask.

I put a finger up. Wait.

I wanted my brother to dance with me, but he pulled me back out of the willow-tree umbrella, into the evening light and said for me to *shush*, that we should go, leave them alone. But I shook my head, I wanted to watch at least one song. Plus, I told him, we got to get dad down.

So I crept back in the dark and lay on my stomach in the cold grass, chin in my hands, and watched my father swinging. He had no control and my mother had to lead like my brother had said but even then, when she was every day disappearing, diminishing, she held their dancing ground. She didn't float like she did with Janet all those years before, but still she closed her eyes and put her head against my father's chest. He stroked her hair and held her tight and then, even in the shiver of candlelight, her face was finally still. They hung there together like the willow boughs themselves and I thought my father looked like an angel, come to carry her away but for her feet, reaching down like roots.

It was that night, I tell them, that I thought maybe my mother wouldn't die, and she didn't, at least not that year or even the year after. She got better.

The dancing machine saves lives! the kids suddenly yell; they are up now.

I shake my head, That is not the point. But they have abandoned the beans and are dancing around the table like strange birds. Hush now, I say, but they are paired off now, dancing together, one in a chair, one standing, cooing fake child love.

Suddenly the oldest stands on a chair. Wait, he puts his hands to his head.

What happened to the eye? Danny's eye? And they all halfway sit again.

I shrug.

Maybe the artist has it, they say, picking up stray beans off the table and putting them back in the bowl like they know they're supposed to.

It's possible, I say, and I don't tell them that a year or so after the dancing machine, Danny put a gun into his empty eye socket and fired, so it didn't matter that I didn't have it.

I guess we could ask him.

I didn't mean to lose it, I tell them.

If it were ours, they say, we would never have lost it.

I know, I say and lay a hand on my eyes so that I can see my mother again, floating and rooted.

It could prove your story true, they say. We could pass it around when we gave our report.

Well, I shrug again.

Now we'll have to make a PowerPoint, one moans.

They look hopeless.

Can we at least take the beans? The oldest one asks.

Yes, I tell them, but then you can't come back. As I say it then, I mean it.

So they gather the beans into their pockets, spilling them and picking them up over and over again until they finally run out of the front door, leaving it open to the daylight like a gaping mouth.

I sit inside in the dim like a tooth, smooth faced.

Two weeks later, they're throwing coins at my door and chanting, Boom-box, boom-box, while I am still dreaming of milk and bones and ropes and all that means nothing to them without the eye itself.

Acknowledgments

*T*hank you to the following presses, and their editors, where many of these stories appeared originally: *Grist* ("Cavalier Presentation of Heartbreaking News"), *mojo* ("Warning Signs"), *Alice Blue Review* ("Time Just Isn't That Simple"), *Oyez Review* ("Fucking Aztecs"), *South Dakota Review* ("In July Flags Are Everywhere" and "Frog Prince"), *The Black Herald* ("American Family Portrait, Clockwise from Upper Right"), Santa Fe Writer's Project *Quarterly* and *SFWP Annual* ("Dementia, 1692"), *Slush Pile Magazine* ("The Crossword"), *COG* ("American Grief in Four Stages"), *The Fabulist* ("Origins"), *South Carolina Review* ("Extra Patriotic").

When I think about all the people who shored me up while I wrote these stories, I am humbled. Thank you to Melanie Rae Thon, Joe Wenderoth, Lucy Corin, Pam Houston, Lance Olsen, Scott Black, Karen Brennan, Rachel Branwen Thomas and Madison Smartt Bell for their early and continued support of my work. Thank you to the University of Utah English Department for providing a community in which this collection could grow. Thank you to Abby Freeland for *seeing* this book and the editorial team at West Virginia University Press for making the book its best. Thank you to my current colleagues at University of Louisiana at Lafayette for all they do to support creative work and the time to do it. Thank you to my students who constantly remind me to doggedly pursue my own work despite a million other things to do. Thank you to the Odd Broads, and I hope I get to join you to talk about this one over mimosas if you deem it worthy. Thank you Mom, Dad, Noah, Anne, Ella, Sam, Quinn, Lynne, Hillary, and Dave for being such a loving family. Thank you Aubrey Andrus, Rosemary Winters, Tyler Anderson, Andrew Smith, Charlie Kimball, Lynne and Dan Levinson, Lynne Whitesides, and Lauren and Jason Morphew for being another family. Thank you to Asia who keeps my feet warm while I write. Thank you to Anaïs, who makes me laugh and keeps me honest, Emile for being my lucky charm, and Marc, thank you for being the first reader on all of these pieces, for always offering me unflagging support, and for knowing exactly what to say even if that's sometimes nothing.

And to all of my loved ones who have lost deeply and endured with a grace beyond measure: you have taught me that life is not for the faint of heart.

This book is for you, too.

Thank you, thank you, thank you.

CPSIA information can be obtained
at www.ICGtesting.com
Printed in the USA
FFHW020055081019
55416527-61181FF

9 781949 199215